The
McKENZIE
ARTIFACT

ALISON KENT

KENSINGTON PUBLISHING CORP.
http://www.kensingtonbooks.com

"Dr. Jones. Again we see there is nothing you can possess which I cannot take away. And you thought I had given up."

—Paul Freeman as Dr. Rene Belloq to Harrison Ford as
 Dr. Indiana Jones in *Raiders of the Lost Ark,* 1981
 (George Lucas, Philip Kaufman, Lawrence Kasdan)

The
McKENZIE
ARTIFACT

One

The drapes drawn open over the motel room's window, Eli McKenzie stood and stared through the mottled glass, squinting at the starburst shards of sunlight reflected off the windshields of the cars barreling down Highway 90 in the distance.

Second floor up meant he could see Del Rio, Texas, on the horizon. And to his left, a silvery sliver of the twisting Rio Grande, a snake reminding him of the venom he'd be facing once he harnessed the guts to cross the river that divided barren desert from civilization.

The room's cooling unit blew tepid air up his bare torso, making a weak attempt at drying the persistent sheet of sweat he wore these days. Sweat having less to do with the heat of the day than with the choking memory of the poison he'd unknowingly ingested on his last trip here.

An accidental ingestion. A purposeful poisoning.

Someone in Mexico wanted him dead.

The only surprise there was that no one but Rabbit knew Eli's true identity. Wanting to dispose of an SG-5 operative was one thing, but he knew he hadn't been made. And that meant this was personal.

This was about his covert identity as a member of the security team guarding the Spectra IT compound across the border. An identity he'd lived and breathed for over a month until the nausea and dysarthria, the diarrhea, ataxia, and tremors turned him into a monster.

One everyone around him wanted to kill.

He'd tried himself. Once.

Rabbit had stopped him and sent him back to New York and Hank Smithson, the Smithson Group principal, to heal, to recover, to find his head and screw it on straight. Eli owed both men his life, though it was his debt to Hank that weighed heaviest.

Hank, who plucked men in need of redemption off their personal highways to hell and set them down on roads less traveled. Roads that took the SG-5 operatives places not a one of them wished to see again once they'd reached the end of a mission's line.

Places like the Spectra IT compound in the middle of the Chihuahuan desert in the state of Coahuila, Mexico.

Scratching the center of his chest, Eli shook his head and pondered his immediate future. He and Rabbit were the only ones inside the compound not working for Spectra. Outside was a different story.

And there had been one person nosing around and causing enough scenes to make a movie.

Stella Banks.

Stella Banks with her platinum blond hair and battered straw cowboy hat and legs longer than split rail fence posts. She was an enigma. A private investigator who dressed like a barrel racer and looked like a runway model.

She kept an office in Ciudad Acuña, another in Del Rio. He knew she was working the disappearance of her office manager's daughter, Carmen Garcia. The girl was fourteen, and like so many of the others gone missing along the border, a beauty.

Unfortunately, she'd also been among the number held inside the compound, waiting to be shipped out and forced into a life of prostitution courtesy of Spectra IT. It was too late for Carmen, but not for the others.

The objective he now shared with Rabbit was to slam the lid on the operation before the next group of twenty girls was scheduled to ship out. And to do that, Eli had to suck it up and cross.

The room wasn't getting any cooler, the day any longer, the truth of what lay ahead any easier to swallow. Like it or not, it was time to go. Once over the border, he'd make his way south and west a hundred or so kilometers in the heap Rabbit had left parked in a field west of the city.

As much as Eli longed for a haircut and a shave, he wouldn't bother with either. The scruffy disguise went a long way to helping him blend in, to hiding the disgust he never quite wiped from his face.

Considering the condition of the car and the roads, he was looking at a good two hours plus of travel time. One hundred twenty minutes to go over the plans he'd worked out with Rabbit to take down these bastards.

Plans trickier than Eli liked to deal with but which couldn't be helped. Not with the lives of twenty teenaged girls on the line.

His plans for Stella Banks he hadn't quite nailed down. He needed her out of the way.

Before he got rid of her, however, he had to find out what she and her outside sources could add to what Rabbit had learned on the inside.

Only then would Eli make certain she never interfered in his mission again.

The car ended up looking worse than Eli expected. Bald tires, oxidized paint, cracked weather stripping, cracked glass. Busted headlights, missing taillights, a crushed rear quarter panel, a gaping hole where there once was a grill.

Thankfully, the grease and grime beneath the hood were only for show. The engine fairly purred. He bounced and jolted his way along the edge of the Chihuahuan Desert, gulping down as much dust as bottled water, glad he was making this trip now instead of during summer's hell.

If he could be glad about anything.

This assignment was closing in on six months. Half a year of his life. One hundred eighty-plus days on his own. It was the first time anything he'd done for Hank Smithson had taken him away from the camaraderie of the Smithson Group, and he was ready to be done.

The support system was still there, the backup, the all-for-one mentality. But with two thousand miles stretching between Mexico and the Manhattan ops center, he felt like the proverbial island no man was.

At least he had Rabbit.

Harry van Zandt, a recent SG-5 recruit, had been sent in at Eli's request when he realized he was losing his mind. Harry's specialty was disguise, blending into the landscape, hiding in plain sight. He hated the nickname Rabbit.

And with just cause, Eli readily admitted as the compound came into view.

The buildings sat along the edge of an arroyo, above a dry creek bed, and inside a twelve-foot chain-link security fence. There was no electrical current flowing through. There was, however, barbed wire looped along the top.

The structures were a mixture of serviceable, crude, and *Saddamized.* As in, the bad guys got the cool stuff. The peons got the crap. Eli and Rabbit both ranked in the middle, meaning they got four walls, a roof, and electricity via generators—as well as access to the girls.

Neither of them wanted the access but knew turning it down would mark them. It was a fine line they walked. And a very big part of the reason Eli had played patty cake with the hands of insanity. An even bigger part of why he was back to face it all again.

The girls were all that mattered. Getting them out of

Spectra's hands and back to their families. He slowed at the checkpoint outside the front gate, saluted the guard there who took a few seconds to recognize him before grinning broadly and waving him through.

Eli waved back, gunned the engine, left rooster tails of chalky red dust in his wake. His cover story was that he'd been called away on another Spectra assignment, one which he'd just completed, one which would elevate his standing as a syndicate insider within the compound.

One for which the Smithson Group had manufactured a complete body of evidence. That, at least, the explanation of his absence, made his return more palatable. There would be no looking over his shoulder. No risk of exposure snapping at his heels.

Winding up this scenario shouldn't take more than a few days, he mused, heading for the main security office and pumping the brakes until the car slid to a stop. The engine might've been a kitten; the brake pads and rotors were shot. Rabbit had taken reality a long step too far.

And speaking of Harry . . .

Having killed the engine, Eli looked up through the half moon cleared by the wiper blades in the dirt coating the windshield in time to see his SG-5 colleague step through the security office's open front door.

Harry wore green fatigues and black combat boots, his feet braced wide, an automatic rifle slung over his shoulder, his hands cupping the flame as he brought up a match to the cheroot held between his teeth. He'd let his hair and beard grow, as had Eli. The two of them looked as unkempt as the locals who worked the compound for Spectra.

Eli had climbed from the car and slung his duffel over his shoulder by the time Harry made it from the warped wooden porch to the ground. Eli shook the other man's hand. "I'd say thanks for the ride, but that car's a piece."

"Got you here, didn't it?"

As if that was saying much of anything, Eli thought, slamming the car's front door. "Always looking on the bright side, aren't you?"

Rabbit blew out a smoke ring and snorted. "Ain't been no sunshine since you been gone, bro."

Eli turned, took in the whole of the compound. The place hadn't changed since he'd been gone except to grow even more dreary-looking, more steeped in the colors of despair and desolation, abandoned, forsaken, dead.

And then he saw her. Locked inside a second cage built beside the one where the girls were kept, a three-sided tar paper shelter for privacy.

A fenced enclosure within a fenced enclosure. No better than a chicken coop or a puppy mill pen.

Stella Banks.

He bit off a string of curses, turned his back to the woman, and faced Rabbit again. Dipping his chin to stare at his partner from over the frames of his sunglasses, Eli asked, "You want to tell me what's up with that?"

"Yeah. Figured that was one surprise best seen first-hand."

"You're just full of good cheer today, aren't you?"

"Doing my best to keep up your spirits."

"Thanks, man. But I'm good. No more going off the deep end. We've got too much work to do."

"More than you can possibly imagine."

"So, fill me in." When Rabbit took a moment to glance beyond Eli's shoulder toward Stella, Eli groaned. "Don't tell me. The more I don't want to imagine has to do with the cowgirl over there."

"You know what they say. Into every life a little rain must fall."

Eli snorted. "I don't recall signing on for this particular deluge." He shook his head, stared down at the orange dust already covering his boots. His quick in-and-out plans to destroy this operation had just been thrown a mighty big wrench.

Er, make that . . . wench.

"Let me guess," he said, turning to lean back against the car. "She either put her foot too close to Ramon's line in the sand, or shoved it heel-deep into her big mouth."

"A little of both, actually," Rabbit said under his breath as footsteps sounded on the porch behind him.

"Elias. Welcome back." The greeting was delivered by Ramon Gutierrez, the local law enforcement officer Spectra had put in charge of the compound.

Essentially, Eli's boss.

Eli pushed away from the car and moved forward. "It's good to be back, Ramon."

"Ah, you missed our heat and drought and dust, I am right, *sí*?" Ramon took Eli's hand between both of his and pumped as if he could bring up stores of information. "Or was it the selection of girls that you missed?"

Eli joined with Harry to laugh at Ramon's implication, wondering if the pompous Latino could hear the strain in their voices. Or if the egotistical ring of his own was too deafening.

Pulling his hand free from the other man's grip, Eli gestured toward the cage with a lift of his chin. "I see the girls have a new den mother."

Ramon followed Eli's gaze across the compound's yard, stepped back and spat on the ground. "*Punta*. She has made my life hell with her snooping."

Yeah. She'd done that to Eli, too. But snatching her up hardly served the Spectra cause. Unless . . .

His gut grabbed hard and knotted tight. "What are your orders? You shipping her out end of month with the girls?"

"Ah, no. Señorita Banks will be receiving a much more personal treatment."

"How so?" Eli asked, his ears pricking as Rabbit crossed

in front of him and muttered, "This is what I was trying to tell you."

The smile that spread over Ramon's face was venomous enough to send a shot of foreboding straight to Eli's heart. "Warren Aceveda?"

Eli nodded. "Spectra's new frontman."

"*Sí.* He is en route. Inspecting the various operations now under his domain."

"And he's interested in the Banks woman?"

"Oh, more than interested, Elias. He has seen her photo. And he plans to take her off our hands and sell her to the highest bidder."

Eli gulped down the lump of hatred lodged at the base of his throat. "That's one way to teach her a lesson."

"It is, *sí*," Ramon went on. "But it is only one."

At Eli's side, Harry cleared his throat. Eli heeded the warning, braced himself accordingly. "Sounds like you have another."

Ramon clapped his hands, rubbed them together. "We were simply waiting for your return, Elias. And now that you are back, the fun can begin."

"Fun?" Eli let his gaze slide from Ramon's to Rabbit's.

"We're calling it Stella Roulette. A spin of the wheel, and bang!"

Two

He was alive.

And he was back.

That sonofabitch was back.

Stella Banks curled her fingers through the chain links of the fenced enclosure and stared.

She couldn't believe it. Not after all the trouble she'd gone through—and gotten into—to get rid of his sorry kidnapping ass for good.

Next time she'd forgo the poison and use a bullet instead.

Not that his being gone from the compound had particularly worked in her favor. But the idea that she had purged the world of one member of this scum-sucking bunch of kidnappers had allowed her to fall asleep with a smile on her face.

Now she slept with one eye open, or she didn't sleep at all. And she knew the result was showing. She couldn't see the color of the puffy half-moons underneath her eyes; she had no mirror, after all. But she could definitely see the puff.

All she had to do was look down and her line of sight was blocked by more than her nose. Ugh. At least they'd left her with her straw hat; as battered as it was, it did offer some protection from the sun.

Though why she was concerning herself with the condition of her skin when it was her life and not her complexion on the line was really rather ridiculous.

At that thought, the one about her life, Stella breathed deeply and sighed. The links in the fence around which she'd curled her fingers bit into her flesh. She held tight anyway, and strained to hear the conversation between the compound's director, *him*, and the man they all called Rabbit.

The distance was too far, the mechanic working on the Jeep between here and there too noisy. She couldn't hear a word. At one point, she would've thought just as well. Being left in the dark about her fate would mean passing the time until the fall of the ax in ignorant bliss.

This was not that point.

Being ignorant now meant being dead. Or worse. Waking up one morning to be shipped off into a life of slavery and prostitution. No. Not a life. An existence at best.

She laughed harshly under her breath. And people thought such happened only in Bruce Willis and Quentin Tarantino movies. That the stories of teen girls disappearing from Mexico's border towns was all hype—hype and rumor intended to discourage Texas's spring-breakers from debauching the local teens as well as themselves.

She sighed again, grimaced against the stabbing pain deep in her belly. Guilt slicing through her bowels, knife-sharp, serrated, a blade sawing her in two.

If she hadn't been of the same mind-set regarding her housekeeper's daughter, she would've put more effort into searching for Carmen Garcia, and ignored the evidence that pointed to the girl having crossed the border with a group of kids returning to Austin and UT.

Ignoring and ignorance, Stella mused. Two words that encompassed her failure. The Garcia girl was still missing, and now here she herself was, caged like a rat despite all her outrage.

She focused on the trio of her abductors again in time to see Rabbit and Ramon heading through the door of the compound's security office. Her gaze locked with that of the third man.

Elias.

She'd been held here now for two weeks; he'd been gone from the compound since early last fall. She'd watched him for a long time during her initial surveillance once she'd discovered the compound's existence.

Three times a day he'd paced the perimeter fence, a rifle slung over his shoulder, a bottle of water in his hand. He kept a cooler at the far back corner of the compound's fence, making it easy for her to slip up the bank of the arroyo and inject the poison unseen.

She hadn't particularly wanted him dead. She'd merely wanted him gone. He'd been the biggest obstacle to her attempts to stake out the compound. Stupid, of course, trying to do it all on her own.

But she knew quite well that corruption ran rampant among the local authorities. Knew, too, that the Feds had no jurisdiction here and wouldn't without evidence of American girls being endangered, as well.

"Got one now, don't we?" she muttered to herself. An all-American girl. A blond, blue-eyed South Texas native with bags under her eyes the size of the Lone Star State.

Her gaze still inexplicably drawn to the man across the yard, she realized the buzz in the compound the last couple of days must've been in anticipation of his return. She'd felt it in the air, seen it in the uncharacteristic burst of activity. Even the girls being held in the fenced-off cell had been forced to clean their quarters—and themselves.

Their universal enjoyment in being given new clothes, soap, shampoo, and makeup would've been cute—if it hadn't been so horribly sad. It was as if they had grasped at any distraction, any small thing to take their minds off their fate.

Stella had yet to discover her own. She doubted it would be any less brutal than that of the girls, but her ignorance of the situation had her imagining the gamut from deliverance to death.

The only thing she'd never considered, however, was that her own demise would hinge upon *his* return. But now? With the way he was looking at her? The reality of the moment seized her. The man, the very man she had done her best to dispose of, was either going to save her or send her further to hell.

And then, while she watched, he tossed his duffel bag onto the hood of the car in which he'd arrived and headed her way.

He walked like one-foot-in-front-of-the-other was his favorite means of transportation. As if he didn't get the chance to use his body, stretch his muscles, put his tendons and joints through their paces as often as he liked. He rolled from his hips when he walked, his gait showing off a long, rangy body that would've had her swallowing with lust if he hadn't been the bad guy.

She swallowed anyway, kept her grip on the fence, watched as he shoved his fists into the pockets of the olive drab fatigues he wore. The motion pulled his black T-shirt tighter over his shoulders. The fit showed off exactly how much weight he'd lost. His waistband rode low on his stomach, which appeared almost concave behind the washboard of his abs.

She was seeing too much, noticing too much, but he'd captured her gaze and refused to release it. She had no strength to fight back. His dark hair was wildly unkempt. It hung in shaggy waves over his nape, skimmed his shoulders. The wind whipped it back, exposing his ears. A glimmer of silver winked in one lobe.

The closer he got, the harder time she had deciding if it was his mouth or his eyes keeping her there. His beard wasn't but a few days old; she imagined it would be coarse and prickly, not yet long enough to have softened. His lips, even pressed together as they were, grim, determined . . . disturbed, were nothing if not kissable. A ridiculous sentiment under the circumstances, but there it was.

She hadn't yet decided on the color of his eyes. And it didn't appear as if she'd have the chance now since, three feet from stopping, he replaced the sunglasses he'd pulled off when talking with the other two men.

He stopped inches away, the chain link fence suddenly seeming like a really good idea. Especially when he braced his forearm against it over her head and leaned down.

"We need to talk."

What she needed was to get out of here. What she was going to do was play it by ear. Refusing his "request" would be stupid. For one thing, he did call the shots.

For another, she was all about information, gathering what she could to free herself, the girls, and bring down these goons.

She narrowed her eyes, squinting up at him. "Talk about what?"

He hesitated answering; even though his eyes were hidden, he tilted his chin enough that she knew he'd looked away. She studied the set of his jaw, the pulse ticking at his temple behind the pewter earpiece of the glasses he wore.

It occurred to her then that this was the closest she'd ever been to him. In the past, she'd watched him from a distance. She'd known his schedule, recognized his walk, learned to distinguish the timbre of his laugh above those of the rest of his cronies.

Being this near to him now, however, she sensed a restlessness in him which seemed at odds with the relief she would have expected of a man returning from the grave.

"You've been away," she finally said when the tension continued to heighten.

He didn't smile, but almost. "You noticed."

"Sure I did. Made it easier to go about my business."
Besides, if I don't miss my guess, I was the one responsible for you leaving.

He looked back at her then. "And what business is that?"

"None of yours," she answered. And then it hit her. That strange *something amiss* she'd been turning over and over, looking for a handle to grasp.

"You don't have an accent. You speak all-American English." Her pulse picked up, her chest tightened. "You're not Hispanic at all, are you? You're as American as I am."

This time his hesitation was brief. He pushed his sunglasses to the top of his head, catching back his shaggy hair and revealing eyes of sky blue. She rattled her cage with a loud growl, pushed away from the fence, and backed toward the tar paper hut in the corner of her cell.

Duped. She'd been royally duped. She'd thought all this time that she was simply dealing with a local, one she had to use her own wits and resources to get out of the way. If she'd known he was American, she could've gone to the authorities in the States, filled them in on what she'd learned about the border kidnappings.

With a U.S. citizen involved, the law enforcement agencies on this side of the border would not have been so quick to turn a blind eye at the first sign of a bribe.

She heard the chain links rattle, glanced up to see him shoving a key into the lock that kept her prisoner. She should run, *run*, bolt through the gate the second it opened, catch him unawares. Her truck was still—hopefully—parked only two miles away.

A quick glance assured her there was no one but the mechanic around. It was now or never. She dried her sweaty palms on her thighs, took a step forward, waited, waited, and ran.

* * *

Eli sensed movement just as he pulled the lock free. He dug the edge of his boot into the ground at the base of the gate, braced his thigh and hip against the galvanized aluminum frame, and held on.

The impact of her shoulder with his ribs sent her stumbling backward with a loud grunt. He grit his teeth against the pain from the blow to his midsection and opened the gate to step inside the cage. He didn't bother locking up. She wasn't going anywhere if she wanted to stay alive.

Walking toward her, he bounced the heavy lock in his palm once, then curled his fingers around it, making a fist. "Are you done acting like you don't have a brain in your head? What the hell did you think you were going to do if you got by me?"

"Run," was all she said.

He backed her up into the center of the cage, halfway to the wall of the structure Ramon's men had thrown together and called shelter.

"Run," he echoed, shaking his head. "You have a particular destination in mind?"

"Yeah," she spat out. "Across the border and into the country where we both belong."

"Assuming a lot, aren't you?"

"What? Are you denying that you're American?"

He wasn't denying anything, but he wasn't yet ready to reveal who he was. And so he lied. "Ramon knows who I am, where I come from, where my loyalties lie."

"What a load of crap. The fact that you're here doing what it is you're doing proves you don't know diddly squat about loyalties."

Her hair was a silver blond mess of windblown strands beneath her hat of crushed straw. Her cheeks and the tip of her nose were pink from the sun. The jeans and boots she wore were filthy from the dust blowing through the compound.

The fact that she'd mashed her lips together to seal in her hatred didn't stop him from thinking about her mouth. And her eyes weren't giving him any easier of a time. They were a crystal clear green and as sharp and smart as he'd seen outside of the SG-5 or Spectra ranks in a very long time.

She had the same snap he and his partners relied on to get out of scrapes. The same snap Spectra used too often to elude the Smithson Group's grasp.

"The only thing here suspect is you. Trespassing and unlawful surveillance aren't going to earn you more badges for your Girl Scout sash," he said, spouting nonsense but with a reason.

"I'll cop to the trespassing, but unlawful surveillance? According to what law? The one you're using to keep me in here? Or the one giving you the right to snatch those girls out of their homes and sell them on the streets?"

She shoved her index finger into the center of his chest and poked hard. "Let me tell you this, mister. There's no chance in hell your make-believe laws will hold up in any court."

She'd advanced on him while she spoke, her hat pulled low, her chin held high. Her eyes burned with zeal and brimmed with tears. And in that moment, that very moment, he felt the slow oozing return of the disgust that had made him an easy target for annihilation all those months ago.

This time, he was the one who advanced, the one who sent her retreating until her backside hit the wall of her shelter and threatened to take it down. "I'm going to tell you something, sister. I am your one and only hope of getting out of here without becoming the prize in a game of roulette. Now, is that what you want? To let the men in this camp take turns with you until you can't walk for a week?"

The moisture that had been welling in her lower lids spilled. She shook her head, her fists balled tight at her sides. She refused to lift a finger and wipe the trails of tears cleaning the dust and grit from her cheeks.

The show of defiance, of will, of strength was Eli's last straw. This woman had been a holy thorn in his side from day one. But he was not about to sacrifice her to the compound staff of ruthless, amoral, cruel men to facilitate his own mission's success.

He stepped even closer. Inches separated their bodies, but he still felt her heat above that which hung in the air. When he reached up with one hand, she flinched; he shook his head to still her and settled his palm at her nape.

She shivered, and he absorbed what he could of her fear, calming her as Hank Smithson would a filly, settling his lips at her temple, breathing in her scent, learning the feel of her hair, her skin, while gathering up his words.

"Okay, then. You listen to me. You do as I say. Exactly as I say. And maybe, just maybe, we can save your virtue and get these girls back to their families before the next transport arrives to take them away."

Three

Stella did as the man Elias asked and threw together the few items she'd been allowed to keep. A hairbrush, a toothbrush, the extra pairs of panties and socks she always carried in her bag. She'd been stranded on stakeouts often enough that she'd learned never to leave home without them.

This time she'd even packed extra jeans and tops. Unfortunately, her backpack remained under the front seat of her truck—or so she hoped. A hope that extended to wondering if her truck was even where she'd left it. If it was, maybe Elias would sneak her through the compound and back down the arroyo.

Or not.

She stepped back out into the ridiculous heat of the late winter sun. She wouldn't be the least bit put out at leaving this dump, though her state of mind would be much better if she knew his plans. Still, she doubted anything he might do could possibly be as frightening as what he'd described.

Until now, she'd been able to hold down the cocktail of fury and fear she'd swallowed at his earlier threat. But now, finding him waiting for her, sunglasses again covering his eyes, brows frowning, mouth grim, the reality of her situation roiled through her like Amistad Dam's spillway. She pressed a fist high into her stomach, looked up and caught his gaze.

"I think I'm going to be sick."

He indicated her shelter with a lift of his chin. "Take care of it here before we get to my place."

"Your place?"

He cocked his head to one side. "Where did you think I was going to take you?"

She hated that her voice trembled. "I thought you were going to let me go."

He laughed then, a sound that spun like blender blades in her stomach. "You came up with that based on something I said?"

She shook her head, furious at his condescension, furious at herself for believing him a savior with a heart. "You said you wanted to get the girls back to their families."

He took hold of her upper arm, a jailer leading his prisoner from her cell. "Letting you go would do nothing but cast suspicion on me. You want the girls freed? We have to make sure the spotlight shines elsewhere."

He kicked the gate closed behind them and propelled her across the yard. "Is that why you made the prodigal son entrance you did? To keep everyone's attention off you?"

"The buzz of my return is nothing compared to the news that's about to get out."

She stumbled, found her footing. "What news is that?"

"The organization employing Ramon is sending in their new front man."

"And why are you telling me all this?" she muttered gruffly, uncertain whether she'd really been rescued or thrown deeper into the pit.

"Because I'm pretty damn sure we're on the same side here."

"And you need an ally."

"No. I need you to stay out of my way."

"Who the hell *are* you?"

"If you don't do what I say, I'll be your worst nightmare. Until then, I'm the best damn hope you have of living to tell your grandchildren about this adventure."

They'd reached the compound's main building then, the one housing Ramon's office, the security and communications centers. She'd seen the inside only briefly the night she'd been hoisted bodily out of her hiding place and unceremoniously dumped—binoculars and all—into the bed of a compound pickup.

This time, at least, she was powered by her own two feet, if not spurred on by the hand holding her arm. The plank flooring echoed hollowly as they walked through the front room that made her think of a teacher's lounge, and headed for the principal's office, ignoring the whispering and snide looks from the staff along the way.

Ramon looked up from his computer monitor, the state-of-the-art equipment set up on a folding table, and got to his feet behind the makeshift desk once he registered that Elias wasn't alone.

Stella took more than a bit of pleasure at seeing the compound director at a loss for words. But then Ramon Gutierrez smiled, a stretch of his thin lips that held enough bad B-movie intent to start the juices in her stomach churning again. His follow-up laughter lit the flame on top. She swore she was going to puke.

"You want me to call in the rest of the men, Elias? You appear anxious to get the games underway," he fairly snarled. "Though I can empathize with the need for recreation considering all that you've recently endured."

And endured at her hands, Stella realized with a gulp.

The look Ramon slid the length of her body had her moving closer to that of her rescuer. She was hot already; the one tiny window unit chugging to cool Ramon's office was wasting its time. But absorbing Elias's warmth was all about safety. She suddenly understood his warnings all too clearly.

Getting out of here alive was the least of her problems. Surviving while inside, enduring what was thrown her way . . . the prize in a game of roulette? The thought had her biting down hard to keep her teeth from chattering and giving away the reality of the fear she was feeling.

"There's been a change of plans, Ramon. She's not up for grabs. She's mine."

Stella stared down at the planks beneath her feet, seeing the shadowed ground, the rocky dirt and dust visible between the flooring's gaps. It wasn't until Ramon came out from behind his desk that what Elias had said sunk in.

She was his. He wasn't going to let her become a victim of a gang rape because he was going to take care of that himself. This unholy alliance she'd been dragged into had just taken a very ugly turn.

"I'm not sure I can allow that, Elias," Ramon was saying when Stella finally found her control and looked up. "The men have been waiting, and now wish to celebrate your return."

Elias shook his head. "It's my return, my celebration. And you have Aceveda to consider."

Stella watched the shift in Ramon's demeanor. The once pompous ass momentarily took on the look of a boy fearing the sting of a switch. The expression flashed and was gone.

But she'd been watching, and she'd seen it. The threat of this Aceveda person was real. It might save her now, but she feared the worst should she still be here when he arrived. For all Ramon's arrogant pomposity, the fact that he feared this other man scared her half to death.

"As much as it pains me to admit it, you are right," Ramon said.

Stella breathed a sigh of relief.

Ramon continued. "Warren will not want his newest acquisition ruined before he arrives to take possession."

This time Stella didn't breathe at all.

"Don't worry," Elias said, taking her by the arm again and backing her out of the room. "I won't use her harshly."

After the morning he'd had, Eli expected to have to drag Stella kicking and screaming across the yard to his barracks, but she walked with him more or less willingly, silent all the way.

He appreciated both, and used the time to figure out what he was going to do with her now that he had her because tying himself to her had never been part of his plan.

Then again, his plan was fairly nonexistent. He'd been playing it by ear since arriving, waiting for a chance to talk in depth with Rabbit after seeing the state of Ramon's little union.

Finding Stella caged like a lioness was a wrench Eli had not been expecting to dodge. Neither was the impending arrival of Warren Aceveda—a tidbit Rabbit should have relayed to the SG-5 ops center. Eli's priority now was to find out why that hadn't yet happened.

Harry might be new on the job, but his job was being a Smithson Group operative. And the information network of the SG-5 machine had not yet plugged into Aceveda's movements as far as Eli knew. With Harry's help, they could have. Unless he'd been in the dark as to the details, hearing them this morning for the first time, too.

The barracks the men shared were built behind the command center and faced the compound's back fence. The building was one long structure divided into equal twelve-by-twelve boxes, the rooms barely large enough for two people, much less the three Eli's would now hold.

The men also shared a community outdoor shower which was no more than a shower head suspended above a concrete pad. No privacy fence meant no privacy. He wondered how Stella was going to react to that. Or if she would insist on the same buckets of water the girls used to bathe.

He guided her up the stairs, down the length of the porch to the last door on the left, assuming the room he shared with Rabbit would still be where he'd left it. It was, evidenced by finding Rabbit inside shoving his few possessions into his duffel.

"This way," Eli ordered Stella, sitting her down on the edge of his bed. She plopped into place and he turned fifty percent of his attention to Harry. "Where are you going?"

Harry jerked his chin to the right. "There's an empty room four doors down. This one isn't going to hold up well beneath the weight of three people."

"You're American, too," Stella said out of nowhere, causing Eli's eyes to click as they rolled back into his head. This woman was going to be his death.

"Wait for me on the porch," he said to Rabbit. The other man nodded and left the room with his duffel slung over his back.

Eli turned to Stella. "Take off your boots."

She glared up from beneath the warped brim of her hat. "I thought you said we were on the same side."

He made a "gimme" motion with one hand. "The boots. Now. And don't even think you're going to barrel out the door while my back is turned," he added when the look in her eyes grew calculating. "For one thing, you've seen the last of my back. For another, Rabbit's right outside the door."

"Right. Your American friend," she practically snarled, though she did cross one leg over the other and tug the boot from her foot. "I can't wait to get back to the States and turn the both of you in."

He waited for the second boot, not about to engage her in any conversation having to do with his mission's endgame and who would be the ones she would be turning in. SG-5 never took credit for the work they did.

But right now, he couldn't explain any of that or the part in his plan she would eventually play.

Right now, he needed her secured so he could talk to Rabbit. Her second boot was barely off when he snatched it out of her hand, grabbed the ankle of the foot on the floor, and locked her into the leg iron welded to his bed frame, which was bolted into the floor.

He listened to her hiss and spit and growl behind him as he walked out the door, her boots in his hand. He motioned for Rabbit to follow him off the porch and out into the compound's yard. The other man dropped his duffel bag in front of the fourth door down and did.

Eli stopped and stared off into the distance, through the chain-link fence that fairly disappeared in the landscape of the Chihuahuan Desert. It was a rugged land, harsh and beautiful. He'd always been more at home in the Great Southwest than at Hank's place in Saratoga, New York. And he hated to admit he'd missed the red rocks and blue sky, the warm *pozas* and the colors of yellow and brown that blended seamlessly into a blanket covering everything as far as he could see.

He hated to admit it, but he did. What he hadn't missed was the ugliness behind him marring the view, that of Spectra IT flaunting the basic human rights SG-5 had sworn to uphold even if they stepped outside convention to do so. He looked up then, and met Harry's inquiring gaze.

"What's up with Aceveda showing up here, man? When did that shit go down?"

Harry shook his head. "About thirty minutes before you drove up, bro. Getting word out wasn't going to happen without me on perimeter duty, and I'm not scheduled to relieve Arturo until nineteen hundred hours."

Eli nodded, feeling better about Harry, worse about their situation. "So, we've got what? Two days?"

"Yep." Harry kicked at a dirt clod. "And then the transport is scheduled to show up in three."

"Fuck." Eli shoved a hand back over his head, raking his hair from his face before shoving his fists to his hips. "And now we've got the cowgirl in there to consider."

"You bringing her in on our plans?"

"Do we have a plan?" Eli scoffed.

"Not one that's going to take care of all those birds when we don't even have one stone."

This time Eli chuckled. It came out sounding like manic hysteria. "Has anyone else gotten sick? Any more of my symptoms shown up in anyone?"

Rabbit shook his head. "It was personal, man. Exactly the way you figured. The why is pretty obvious. You got in someone's way."

"I've been in a whole lot of someones' ways since I first showed up. But I was pretty damn sure none of them knew that." After he'd been poisoned, who knew what the hell stupid things he'd said?

But this someone would've been out to get him long before he'd started losing his mind. "Right now, I don't think I've got time to throw out a dragnet and figure it out. We've only got two days to get a dozen scared girls out of here undetected, not to mention the cowgirl in there and ourselves."

The fact that Rabbit was shaking his head so calmly could not possibly be a good sign. Not a good sign at all. Eli didn't want to ask, but he had to know. He had to know.

"What is it?" he asked, feeling the tightness in his jaw work its way the length of his spine.

"It's two dozen girls, Eli. Two dozen girls."

"What? They've never run that many at one time," he said, his pulse thundering in his ears.

"Right. It's Aceveda's doing. The girls arrived this morning. He shut down the Baja facility. The Feds were closing in."

"This was part of your meeting with Ramon this morning?"

Harry nodded.

"Any more good news?" Hell, if this op went any further downhill . . .

Harry nodded.

Eli bit off a curse. "What?"

"Aceveda knows there's a leak. He's bringing in a Spectra agent to check all our backgrounds."

Jesus H. Christ. "Meaning if we're still here when he shows, we're boned."

four

The room was stifling. The jerk had left her to swelter without opening the window high above on the wall or turning on the oscillating fan sitting on the desk which, aside from the beds, was the only piece of furniture in the room. The man apparently lived out of his duffel bag and off the desktop and floor.

The plywood walls were bare. A single bulb screwed into the fixture overhead on the ceiling. The light, she knew from watching the buildings in the dark, would flicker depending on the fuel level in the compound's generator.

The room's two twin beds were pushed against opposite walls with the desk between. The mattress beneath her bottom was thin, as were the sheet and blanket folded and stacked at one end. The bed had obviously not been used during Elias's time away. And now that Rabbit had taken his things and moved out, the room held nothing of interest.

Except, perhaps, the leg iron.

The room had obviously been used as something other than sleeping quarters at some time in the past. She couldn't help but wonder exactly how long this operation had been in business, and who it was behind the whole thing. It wasn't a local enterprise, of that much she was certain.

This area of the country would be hard pressed to find and afford the resources keeping the compound viable. Which meant this area of the country had been chosen because of its inaccessibility and quality of life. No one working here would ever bite the hand feeding them for fear they'd never again see another hand.

That assessment, of course, did not include her new roommate or his ex. Those two were not who they were pretending to be, but taking her discovery to Ramon was hardly in any best interest but his. In fact, there had to be a reason she'd been let in on their secret. Now to find out what they wanted with her and from her—and how to turn the tables.

She was on her hands and knees examining the bed frame's mooring when the door opened and Elias came in. He left it ajar and stepped onto the bed to open the window while she looked up from her place on the floor. Only when he stepped off and down did he seem to realize what she was doing, even though she'd sat back on her heels and done her best to appear innocent.

"You're not going anywhere, so you might as well give it up and save your nails."

She scrunched up her eyes and glared. "Do I look like someone who cares about nails?"

He took three steps in reverse and sat on the edge of the second bed. "What *do* you care about?"

She stared at him across the very squat width of the room. Now that they were out of the sun's glare, free from the wind blowing grit into every crevice and pore, dust into her eyes and her mouth, she took a moment to study more than his looks, which were admittedly good, and made more so by the mystery he was.

She wondered what he was asking her, if he wanted to know more than the simple question implied. The crow's feet at the corners of his eyes ran deep, as did the brackets on either side of his mouth, barely visible beneath his thickening beard. But she could see them, could tell whatever was going on in his mind was much more than the words he had spoken.

She pushed up to mirror his pose by sitting on the edge of the bed and lacing her hands between her spread knees. "Right now, I care more than anything about finding my housekeeper's daughter who has been missing since Labor Day weekend."

"And you think she's here?"

Stella shook her head. Strands of her hair spilled from behind her ears where she'd tucked it. "Not now, I don't. She could very well have been here and been shipped out to God knows where before I ever found this place, though."

"How did you find it?" he asked.

She wasn't yet sure who he was, what side he was truly on, if she could trust him or anything coming out of his mouth. But right now, he was undoubtedly her very best hope.

"A fluke, truly. I'd been checking in with a contact at the airport in El Caballo and was on my way back to my office in Ciudad Acuña. A truck headed in the direction from where I'd come drove by. A dual-axle pickup hauling a gooseneck horse trailer. I wouldn't have paid a bit of attention except I caught a flash of color as it passed.

"When I looked in my rearview, it wasn't a braided tail or mane like I'd thought waving at all. It was a piece of clothing, a skirt or blouse that was caught in the trailer's door. I waited until the truck was almost out of sight and turned around. The driver pulled into the airport just as a small cargo plane landed."

Stella took a breath, stared at her hands, which were now bloodless fists from her fingers clutched so tightly. "I knew I could watch the trailer being unloaded without being seen. But if it did turn out to be girls and not horses inside, a real long shot when I thought about it, I was going to have trouble following the truck without being discovered, considering the terrain. I would've been a sitting duck."

"But it was girls and not horses."

She nodded. "A dozen of them as best as I could count. I stood in the bed of my truck and watched from half a mile away."

"Binoculars? What, Zeiss?"

She nodded. "None of my camera equipment would do me any good from that distance."

"So how'd you make it to this place?"

She backed up along the chain of events. "I honked the driver down as he pulled through the cargo entrance. Fortunately, I had a starburst crack in my windshield."

"Which you accused him of causing."

She nodded. "Thank God for back roads and gravel. Told him it was going to cost me three hundred dollars to fix and he owed me at least half. He couldn't get rid of me fast enough."

"He paid."

"Yep. And I slapped a miniature transmitter inside the wheel well while he was peeling bills from the wad in his pocket," she finished.

When she finally looked up, Elias was nodding as if nothing she'd said came as a surprise. He seemed way too at ease with her investigative machinations, as if he, too, were familiar with tracking systems and lying through his teeth.

Then again, he'd rattled off the brand name of her binoculars without thinking twice. Either he'd seen them after she'd lost them, or he knew the manufacturer's rep. Now she had to consider that nothing he told her was the truth, and that he was weighing every word she said with the same bullshit scale.

And just as the thought crossed her mind, he met her gaze and asked her, "Where do you stand on trust?"

She stared at him for a moment, searching his gaze for some clue as to what he wanted, what he was asking. She got no closer to the truth of the matter this time than she had previously.

So she wiggled her foot and yanked at the chain binding her to the bed. "You said it best. I'm pretty damn sure we're on the same side."

She read the nod he gave her as a silent touché, an acknowledgment that she would not be easily cowed or subdued, that her skills, input, and insight were as vital to their shared agenda as were his.

Then again, she could have been imagining all of that considering he next said, "Then if I ask you to do something . . . questionable, do you think you can do it without asking questions?"

Ah, yes. Women. The mindless sex. She cocked her head, flipped back her hair, blinked several mindless times before answering. "By questionable, I assume you mean sexual?"

"I need a distraction," he said, and he didn't even flinch.

"I see." A distraction. A distraction. From what, to whom, and why? "And what better way to distract a compound staffed by horny Neanderthals than to use me as the bait."

He gave a single nod. "I'm in a bind like you can't believe. I don't have a lot of time to finesse a more subtle plan."

Irony of ironies. The man she'd poisoned to get out of her way was asking for her help. "What do you have in mind?"

Knees spread, he dropped back onto his elbows, tucked his chin to his chest and met her gaze. "Think of it as a shower cam. Minus the camera. And the privacy. And the anonymity. And the paycheck."

"Wow." She widened her eyes appropriately. "You make it sound so appealing."

"I need to make contact with a source on the outside. I

can't do it unless I know the rest of the men will be occu-
pied."

Her thoughts raced. It was bargaining time. Tit for tat—
with the tit part being literal. "You using my sexuality to
get what you want would make you my pimp, right?"

He didn't argue, didn't deny, didn't speak.

"And you being my pimp means I get left behind to fend
off the scum while you make all the profit." Still he said
nothing. "What I'm trying to figure here is what profit are
you making?"

"No profit. No glory. And you won't be left behind."

"Hmm," she mused, as it occurred to her that he had no
idea she was responsible for his recent illness, that he was
bargaining with his own personal devil.

She wondered if he'd be more apt to let her fend for herself if he knew. "So what's the plan?"

He pushed up, sat forward. "The shift change for the
perimeter guard is at nineteen hundred hours."

She knew that. She'd memorized the schedule of the compound's entire security force before being captured. "You
go on duty then, and what? I take a shower?"

"No. Rabbit goes on duty then."

"So, he *is* part of this weird secret conspiracy you've got
going on here."

He didn't respond, simply met her gaze as if waiting to
continue until she'd had her sarcastic say. She rolled her
eyes. Blood from a turnip wasn't half of it. Yet he was the
one spouting off about trust. She waved him on.

"Rabbit goes on duty at nineteen hundred hours," he
said, raking back his hair and dragging both hands down
his face—the first indication of his exhaustion she'd seen.
"He'll make contact with our team, but he needs to be assured of privacy when he calls."

She nearly choked on her skepticism. "Must be one hell
of a satellite service. Not to mention one hell of a phone."

Elias nodded. "One no one in Ramon's employ has been

issued or would have legitimate reason to own. Rabbit gets caught, he's dead meat."

Bobbing her head because she had no idea how to react, Stella finally found her voice. "And where will you be?"

"With you."

"Showering?" she squeaked.

He didn't answer right away. He didn't confirm by nodding or deny by shaking his head. He did nothing but sit and stare into her eyes.

She wouldn't have minded if the truth of what she'd done wasn't running rampant so close to the surface. She feared if she blinked too rapidly and cleared her thoughts, he'd see every detail of what she'd been thinking. Of the poison, the water bottles, how desperately she'd wanted him out of the way.

So she wasn't the least bit prepared to have him lift one dark brow and ask, "Is that what you want? For me to shower with you?"

Her response was an unladylike snort. "Whatever gave you that idea?"

"You did," he finally said, and she realized he was right.

She had been the one to bring it up—not because that's what she wanted, but because the way he'd spoken the words "with you" sounded like that's what he had in mind, especially when she factored in the not-so-subtle invitation of his body. The way he'd leaned back and stared, the way he'd spread his legs and framed her in the wide V as he did, the fit of his clothes in that position leaving nothing to the imagination.

At least not to hers, which was quite appreciative of all he had to offer, even if he had chained her to his bed. "Well, you can think again because that was not my intent."

He shrugged, the motion seemingly careless when she doubted he ever did anything without care. "You say so."

"I do say so, but I would appreciate having you nearby. Preferably with a gun." She wasn't stupid. She knew the sort of distracting act he wanted was an invitation to trouble. "And I won't strip. I'll shower in my underwear, but I won't strip."

He studied her intently, thoughts flashing like road flares in his eyes. He needed her, that much she knew, that much she could tell, but on this she would not budge. Not until he broke down and told her that unless she took off her clothes she would die.

In that case, she'd reconsider her pride and her morals; they wouldn't do her a whole lot of good if she were dead. But right now, right now, such wasn't the case. She wasn't a prostitute. He wasn't her pimp.

When he finally spoke it was only to say, "The water's cold, you know. Straight from the well. It's not the same as warming a bucket in the kitchen."

Obviously a perk only the men were offered; she knew the girls sponged off in cold. "That will make the show even that much better, won't it? Nice, tight headlights with which to blind my audience."

"The long legs and blond hair won't hurt either." He paused, cleared his throat. "I hear there's an ongoing bet in the compound even now."

God, but she was going to be sick. "About me?"

He nodded. "About whether you're a true blonde."

The laughter that bubbled up from her belly tasted like sour milk. "And you were hoping I'd tell you so you'd know how to wager?"

"Something like that."

She got to her feet, prepared to advance, to pounce, caught tight by the iron grip at her feet. The humiliation awaiting her was bad enough. She wasn't about to give him a head start on his right-handed satisfaction.

"Sorry, Elias," she fairly spat. "You'll have to wait and see for yourself."

He rose slowly, his hands on his thighs as he pushed up, his chin lifted, his gaze never once leaving hers. She'd said something wrong, used words he didn't like, a tone he hadn't wanted to hear.

And for the first time since he'd walked into her cage and made her his prisoner, she realized the frying pan truly was a lot safer place than the fire.

"It's Eli," he said. "Not Elias." And then he left the room.

Five

What Eli was asking Stella to do was nothing he'd wish on any woman. The dozen men employed here by Ramon Gutierrez defined the scum of the earth, and had been hired for that very reason. Only Eli and Rabbit had needed to forge cast iron stomachs to live and work here the long months they had.

Not that Eli's forging had done him much good. The poison he'd ingested had seeped straight into his bloodstream. And he still battled the demons hounding and taunting him with the reality that he'd been unable to stop what was happening to the girls.

That fact, more than anything about this op, was what ate at him, clawing through his gut, ripping him open from the inside out until holding down water was the best he could do. Getting beyond the numbers, facing the truth of how many had been shipped out, was not coming easy.

The sacrifice of a few for the greater good had never been an idea he embraced. Not now as an SG-5 operative. Not before when running black ops.

While he and Harry dug beneath the surface of the compound's operation into the global network of Spectra IT's prostitution ring, girls were losing their innocence, their lives. The only upside to the mission's accelerated schedule was the chance to save the girls here now.

Thinking of prostitution naturally brought to mind his role as pimp, and the reason he was here in the supply room checking out a bar of soap, a cake of shampoo, and a towel for Stella to use. She'd called out to him earlier when he'd left, asking for a razor, needing to shave her legs.

He ran his thumb over the twin blades in the cheap disposable, figuring if he kept an eye on her the plus side of the sideshow would be worth the risk of putting a sharp instrument into her hands.

He dropped the four items onto the folding table just inside the door where Carlos, the supply clerk, sat ready to argue that Eli was over his monthly allotment. Or was ready until realizing that in this case the customer was always right.

Still, it was in Carlos's nature to argue, so he did. "Did you return to find your soap and shampoo missing, Elias? My records show you still have—"

"These aren't for me." Time to set the bait.

"Then I cannot issue you—"

"They're for the American woman." Carlos looked up from his ledger while Eli grabbed up the items. "She insists on a shower."

"A shower?" Carlos echoed.

Eli nodded. "Later. It should make for an entertaining show."

"The shower out of doors?"

"I'm pretty sure that's the only one we've got, Carlos." The other man was already starting to drool. Soon he'd be hyperventilating, but would hopefully start the news circulating before he passed out. Carlos was, after all, the compound's worst gossip. "I've got to see Ramon first. But I'll take her down after dinner."

"And we can all observe? Or will this be canceled as was our game of roulette?"

"Observe away, *mi amigo*. Observe away," Eli said, offering the other man a quick playful salute on his way out the door, though he didn't feel the least bit like playing. The seed, however, had been sown, and that was what counted.

Tucking the soap, shampoo, and razor into the pockets of his fatigues, Eli tied the thin towel around his head like a bandanna, the ends trailing down between his shoulder blades, and made his way to Ramon's office.

"Ah, Elias. Finally we have a chance to talk business," Ramon said, as Eli walked in and closed the door behind him. "I'm sorry you had to return and handle a matter of such unimportance."

"If Aceveda is interested in the woman," Eli began, once again employing his Hispanic accent, "then the matter is not insignificant."

"You are correct," Ramon acceded with a nod as Eli took the seat in front of the desk. "The isolated conditions under which we work often cause me to forget that there is, indeed, an authority to whom I must answer."

He made it sound like Spectra IT sat on the right hand of God when they were more the type to operate out of a Jersey warehouse. "Bring me up to date on Aceveda's visit. I was surprised to learn he thinks making a personal inspection is necessary. The job you've been doing here hardly requires monitoring."

Ramon nodded in acceptance of the compliment. "I understand that he felt his predecessor, a Peter Deacon, was focusing too much on the perks of the good life instead of on the organization's interests over which he held charge."

"Power will go to some men's heads," Eli offered, still unclear all these weeks later what exactly the other man knew of the scope of Spectra IT.

"And fortunately, you have returned to assure I do not allow such an occurrence here."

Hands on his knees, Eli leaned forward. "She's a beautiful woman. It's not difficult to understand wanting to give your men a taste of what she has to offer as a reward for the job they've done here."

Ramon leaned back in his chair, braced his elbows on the tattered vinyl arms, and steepled his index fingers beneath his chin. "You are observant as always, Elias. I have missed the subtle guidance of my right-hand man."

"The Rabbit tells me the Baja operation has ceased, and the acquisitions have been transferred here?"

"Yes. Another of Aceveda's managerial decisions. Once he completes his inspection, the next shipment will be made."

"And the supplies? They are holding out with the additional girls? Or should I see to the inventory?"

"No. Carlos was able to arrange for another delivery before the truck's arrival. It has been a busy quarter, Elias. And now the days ahead hold much more work for all of us."

"Then the timing of my return is fortunate."

"It is indeed. Especially as I have a task that will require your assistance."

"Just tell me what it is."

"Aceveda will be bringing another man with him, one I believe is an expert on ferreting out information. He wishes to conduct a rigorous background check on all the men here, and I'd like to offer him your services."

Right. Like this was going to go down well. "Any clue what he's looking for?"

"The organization believes a member of our staff here may not be what he seems." Ramon's expression darkened. "I hate to be the bearer of bad news, Elias, but I suspect that your friend Rabbit may have infiltrated our operation for purposes of personal gain."

Shit. If Ramon had Harry on radar, then keeping his contact with SG-5 tonight under wraps was critical. Eli slowly straightened where he sat. "I have hesitated speaking to you about Rabbit, but I have suspicions of my own."

"Then perhaps the investigation should start with him,

and you can share what you have learned with Aceveda's man."

As if pondering the great wisdom in Ramon's suggestion, Eli nodded. "Has Arturo been scheduling the perimeter patrol in my absence?"

"He has," Ramon said, righting his chair and reaching for a ledger on the corner of his table-cum-desk. "Feel free, however, to make whatever changes seem necessary with our discussion in mind."

"I don't want to engage Rabbit's suspicion, so I'll wait until the morning shift change to implement a new rotation. If I explain the change is to coincide with Aceveda's visit, it should raise no red flags."

"Your logic makes perfect sense. I foresee no objections."

"You may have one."

"Oh?"

"I have arranged a bit of entertainment for the evening, though I want to clear it first with you."

"And what entertainment is that?"

"The woman. Stella. She is demanding a shower. An activity I thought the men would like to watch."

Ramon tossed back his head and laughed. "And yet again we see there is no suggestion I make that you are not able to improve and still execute. Feel free, Elias, to start the show."

By the time nineteen hundred hours rolled around, the word of Stella's Wet 'n' Wild Shower Hour had spread.

The buzz in the compound rivaled that prior to any World Series, Superbowl, or Final Four play-off game. Only the scale was smaller.

One woman, ten men. He hated the odds.

Hated them enough that he'd insisted Ramon demand the men forfeit their weapons to Carlos in the supply center and remain behind the barricade Eli set up.

He sold the idea to the compound director with a liberal use of Aceveda's name, the need to see no harm come to his prized acquisition, and the guarantee of ten front-row seats.

He and Rabbit, of course, would retain their weapons. Rabbit, because he would be on perimeter patrol. Eli, because he was the evening's ringmaster and sole security officer.

Funny how that had worked out.

Now to prep Stella.

He took the two steps onto the barracks porch in one quick leap and made his way to the room they were sharing. Funny how that had worked out, too.

But the accelerated time schedule for shutting down Spectra's holding center, not to mention the unforeseen obstacles lobbed from the right and the left since his arrival this morning, meant combining forces and efforts even if between them there was no love or like lost.

Lust was another matter.

He strode through the door he'd left open earlier only to find Stella asleep. Both of her sock-covered feet were flat on the floor, her knees bent, her back on the bed as if she'd fallen down and hadn't bothered to get up.

He wondered if she'd finally relaxed her guard now that she knew she wasn't working alone, that having a partner— of sorts—with the same goal—more or less—had taken a load off her mind.

What it had done for him was factor in another life to keep out of Spectra's clutches. He would've been much happier working solely with Rabbit, trusting the other SG-5 operative to have his back. Stella was an unknown.

Shipping her out with the rest of the girls, getting her out of his hair, taking down the compound before Aceveda arrived . . . Eli bit off a harsh curse, dragged his hands over his face, stared down at the woman lying in his bed.

If he didn't launch stage one of his weak-as-hell plan, wasn't none of that gonna happen.

He tugged on the chain of the leg iron with the toe of his boot. "Wake up, sunshine. It's show time."

Stella's eyes opened as if she hadn't been sleeping at all. As if she'd been awake while he'd watched her chest—okay, her breasts—rise and fall with her breathing's even rhythm. As if she'd known he'd been thinking about the length of her legs, where her ankles would meet, where her heels would press, if she wrapped him up in her love.

Hell and a half, what was he thinking? She was bossy and ballsy, mouthy and more trouble than he needed. She was not the type of woman even his basest of instincts needed. He'd be too afraid she'd just as soon blow his head off as blow him.

She pushed up onto her elbows, lifted one brow. "I may not be cheap, but I can be had."

"Tell that to your audience," he grumbled, leaning down to unlock the iron from her leg. "They're waiting for the curtain to go up."

"You mean for my clothes to come off," she muttered.

The thought shouldn't have caused his pulse to pick up, but it did. He got to his feet, pulled her towel from his head, her soap, shampoo, and razor from his pockets. Rubbing the circulation back into her ankle, she checked out the supplies he'd placed on the bed.

"I guess it's too much to hope that razor might actually be useful in defending myself."

"Only against the siege ravaging your legs."

She stuck out her tongue as she pushed up to stand. "I've half a mind not to shave, then wait until you're sleeping, sneak into your bed, and order my legs to attack."

He thought again of her legs around his waist, her thighs open, her knees squeezing him tight. He wondered what she'd think if she knew he wasn't repulsed at all but on the verge of being turned on.

He shuffled where he stood, praying Rabbit and Arturo's shift change was in the bag, and that Rabbit was on his way to make the call that would save all of their asses and what remained of Eli's sanity. "Are you ready?"

She shook her head. "I need my boots."

He stepped out onto the porch where he'd left them earlier, stepped back into the room and tossed them to the bed. She sat, tugged them on, grabbed up the rest of her things—including her hat, which she shoved onto her head, pulling down the brim until her eyes were completely hidden.

"Let's go," she said.

Eli moved towards the door and closed it. "Listen. I'll think of something else. Another distraction. It shouldn't take Rabbit long to make his call. Calling off the shower should be distraction enough."

She was silent for a long moment, looking down, either at the floor or the items she held in her hand. He couldn't tell by the set of her shoulders what she was thinking. He couldn't see enough of her face to gauge her expression. The way she was breathing, the color in her skin—neither hinted at her frame of mind, her emotional state, or her mood.

He braced himself in case she charged—through him, the door, the chain-link fence, and out into the Chihuahuan Desert. But she didn't. She finally, simply lifted her chin and met his gaze with a directness, a fierceness he felt all the way to the bone.

"No. I'll do this. I want to make sure there's not a man out there who gives a shit what Rabbit is doing on patrol. I want his call to go through. I want your team to come in and save these girls. But you're going to owe me in a very big way. Remember that, because I will collect."

Six

The only way she would be able to do this was by closing her ears, closing her eyes, and picturing no one but Eli.

Eli. She liked the name. And she was afraid she liked the man. A twisted sort of Stockholm Syndrome, she supposed. Except he wasn't truly holding her prisoner. And he wasn't even the bad guy.

Which meant what she was feeling was more about who she perceived him to be.

He was a man she would be attracted to under any circumstances. He was beautiful to look at, quick-witted and smart, but the fact that he'd been willing at the last minute to let her off the hook said a lot.

A hell of a lot.

He wasn't the cold mercenary type to sacrifice anyone and everyone between here and his cause. She'd known too many men who were, too many causes unworthy of the lives given, too many selfish bastards willing to hurt the ones they supposedly loved for their own gain.

He walked behind her, off to the right, placing himself between her and the leering, jeering bastards comprising her audience. He had a gun, an assault rifle slung across his back. The group watching her had nothing. No handguns, no knives, no weapons of any kind.

It did make her feel marginally better to know he had her back. That she was no longer working alone. That she was, in fact, now part of a team of three.

She set her towel, soap, shampoo, razor, and hat on the fifty-five-gallon drum that would serve as her vanity table. Keeping her back to the men, she stood on one foot then the other to tug off her socks and her boots, determined to keep them dry.

The clothing items joined the rest of her things away from the water that she knew would be cold. And with the sun rapidly setting, well, she was about to lose her one and only heat source, since she refused to leech any of that put off by the nearby crush of male bodies.

Unfortunately, that reality wasn't making her move any faster. Her earlier outburst apparently proved that she was all talk and no action.

Even when Rabbit crossed her line of vision on the first leg of his patrol, reminding her that stripping to her camisole and thong was nothing compared to what she was saving twenty-four girls from having to do . . . even then her fingers still fumbled with the buttons on her blouse.

The wolf whistles and catcalls from the animals at her back hardly helped.

Finally, the buttons slid from their holes, the lapels parted, and the blouse came off. She even got the zipper down on her jeans and managed to skin the denim from her legs. Gooseflesh immediately prickled her skin as waves of nerves and dread consumed her, a big wide pelican beak of a mouth swooping down to swallow her up heart, mind, and soul.

And that was fine. That meant only a shell of who she really was remained behind to perform. A female shell succumbing to timeless instinct, seeking out and attracting the alpha male of the pack.

* * *

He felt as if she were dancing just for him. And it *was* a dance, though performed to no music but that in her mind.

The only sounds audible in the compound yard were those of the running water, the obscenities shouted in the keys of male voices, and the rolling thunder of his pulse in his ears.

It was a wonder he hadn't stroked out dead where he stood. His blood pressure had shot through the top of his head the first time she'd stepped into the water's spray, the sun setting over the desert turning the water beading on her skin into teardrops of gold.

Her body was fiery hot, all long legs and sweet curves that she worked like she'd been dancing in strip clubs since the day she'd been born. No. It went way beyond that. Because none of what she was doing smacked of a jaded detachment.

It was personal, involved, and he felt it like a knife to the gut.

He leaned against the barracks wall, his rifle cradled just threateningly enough that the horny goons watching Stella knew he meant business. He cast his gaze in their direction, assuring himself that none were on the verge of crossing his line—or any line—then looked over their collective heads as Rabbit walked by in the distance.

The other man stopped, lifted his sunglasses, and rubbed the bridge of his nose. The signal. He'd made contact with SG-5. The distraction had worked. Eli should've felt a bolt of relief, returning his gaze to Stella. Instead what he felt was . . . distracted.

Her camisole top was the color of champagne with a soft metallic sheen. The wet fabric clung to her breasts, which were as plump and full as peaches ripe with juice. The scrap of material that served as her panties left her ass cheeks bare and nothing else to the imagination—except whether or not she was a natural blond.

The flesh of her sex beneath her panties was shaved or waxed bare.

His mouth watered, and he loathed the fact that others were watering, too. He wanted perversely to be her sole observer, her one-man audience, the only one who would later know the pleasure of having her in bed.

Thankfully, she appeared to be wrapping things up, rinsing her arms and her legs, having cleaned her lingerie along with the more intimate parts of her body. She leaned forward from the waist, then rose suddenly to toss back her hair, the long, wet, rope-like strands flinging off an arc of water before slapping down into the center of her back.

Sensing movement at his side, Eli shoved off the barracks wall and readied his weapon, stopped in the act of turning by Ramon's hand coming down on his shoulder.

"May I suggest you sleep tonight, Elias, with one foot on the floor and your door double-bolted? I would hate to see any of my men attempt to take advantage of this gift they have been given."

The thought had already crossed Eli's mind tenfold, and he was doubly thankful for the perimeter security and lock on the girls' cage as well. "Trust me. No one will get to her because no one will get through me. She'll be ready for delivery to your boss when he arrives."

"The day after tomorrow. You must keep her safe until then."

It was on the tip of his tongue to argue that she wouldn't have been safe at all if this morning's game of roulette had happened. But he picked that moment to look up. And his world tumbled from Atlas's shoulders.

Holding her clothes tucked into her hat like a bedroll, Stella stood waiting, her hair wrapped in the towel, her limbs dry, her feet once again in her boots.

She wore her wet lingerie like her own skin and a look on her face that said if he didn't get her out of here now, she'd scramble his balls for breakfast.

He crossed the short width of the yard toward her. Behind him, the men dispersed under Ramon's instruction with what Eli hoped was good-natured grumbling and not ill intent.

His own intent was suspect enough. When he stopped, he had a hard time keeping his gaze on her face. "Is there some reason you're not dressed?"

"I'm not putting on my only clothes over underthings that are soaking wet. And I'm not stripping down the rest of the way to do that out here."

"Fine." He took hold of her upper arm. It was bare, damp, and pebbled with cold gooseflesh that had his mind seeing the tight knots of her nipples, had his mouth watering, his cock hardening at the thought of sucking on her and warming them up. "Let's go."

He led her back to the barracks where she stomped up the steps, onto the porch, down to his room and inside.

He followed, but halted at the doorway. "I'm going to talk to Rabbit. Lock yourself in and don't open the door for anyone but me."

She dropped her things on the bed, dug into her bag for a hairbrush and a clean thong. She looped the latter over her wrist while she toweled what water she could from her hair. She then started in on brushing it. She never looked at him, never said a word.

He had a hard time focusing when faced with her nearly naked body and the panties on her arm. "Did you hear anything I just said?"

"I heard all of it. I'm just waiting for you to go."

"Look, Stella—"

"Look, Eli," she interrupted, turning toward him, giving him a full frontal view of her body, the sheer clinging fabric doing little to cover her, the line of her long legs stopped by her boots.

"I would like nothing more than for you to stay and chat, except that would be a lie. What I want is to be alone, to brush my hair, dress, and deal with my humiliation privately. So go and do your thing and don't worry about me."

He didn't even come up with a response before she reached the door and slammed it in his face. He listened for the locks to click into place, and even then he hesitated leaving. Not because he feared for her safety, but because he ached for her humiliation.

He doubted he'd be able to kick his own ass hard enough to pay for what he'd put her through. Reminding himself that he'd given her an out, that she'd been insistent and willing didn't ease the guilt pricking his prick of a conscience.

Involving civilians in any SG-5 op was a risk—to the mission and to the individual. But this was different, an emotional injury resulting in an unseen scar. His impotence left him paralyzed, left him standing and staring at the door she'd shut in his face.

"Shit." He was standing here jerking off to a woman's hurt feelings instead of taking care of business. He glanced quickly at his watch, then headed for the far end of the porch, his steps heavy enough to echo up through the floor where Stella was standing.

Forgoing the stairs, he leapt to the ground and jogged toward the far corner of the perimeter fence obscured by the structure housing the compound's motor pool. Not that the pool ran deep; even adding in the beater he'd driven up in this morning, the vehicles could be numbered using one hand.

He rounded the building, leaned back against it and waited for Rabbit to make his way up from the arroyo. It only took five minutes. Eli walked up to the fence, ready with his story of checking up on the other man should Ramon witness and question their meeting.

"You filled them in on Aceveda's timetable?"

Rabbit nodded, ran a hand over his short dark hair to shake out the sand. "Julian, Mick, and K.J. are in the air.

They'll intercept the transport tomorrow and take the girls out before Aceveda arrives."

"Good, good." The three Smithson Group operatives mentioned wouldn't, on close inspection, pass as Mexican nationals, but Eli knew—and trusted—that his partners would work out their cover.

"It stinks that this is all we're getting out of this." Rabbit sucked back a mouthful of water from his canteen. "We could've closed up shop here months ago."

Months ago, Eli had been fighting the poison in his system. Now he was fighting the clock to avoid an interrogation and the resulting exposure. Bringing down the compound was a small victory in the larger Spectra picture.

But at least they would get out the girls.

And keep SG-5 off the radar.

It wasn't all of what they'd hoped for, but it was good enough for now. "I talked to Gutierrez about the Spectra agent coming in for the background checks. He thinks you're the leak."

Rabbit sputtered his second drink of water. "Me? What the fuck?"

"Exactly," Eli said with a twisted sort of grin. "Welcome to the Smithson Group. Hope you enjoy your stay."

"If Ramon thinks I'm the leak, you know he won't let me leave with the transport. If he lets the transport leave at all." Harry looked out over the desert. "Wasn't Aceveda wanting to check out the girls?"

A hitch. Nothing more. "Give me till tomorrow. I'll figure it out."

"All of it?" Harry asked, glancing back. "Including getting you, me, and the cowgirl outta here?"

Eli pictured Stella wearing nothing but her skin and her boots. He stifled a hell of a groan. "One thing at a time, grasshopper. One thing at a time."

Seven

Stella was asleep when Eli finally knocked on the door. She'd snooped through his things, turned the room upside down and righted it again, done all she could short of dismantling the furniture looking for clues, information, evidence of what he was, who he was working for, why he was here.

Between the emotionally exhausting performance earlier, the relief that had followed once she'd finished, and the adrenaline rush fueling her illegal search, she'd passed out within minutes of lying back on the bed to consider her own strategy should he turn out not to be the answer to her prayers.

When she heard the knock, it was apparent it wasn't the first time he'd rapped on the door. She'd been dreaming fierce dreams about a wild-eyed warrior who'd saved her from a band of club-wielding outlaws and claimed as his prize her virtue. It was the beating of the clubs she'd thought she was hearing, and she came awake startled to find herself alone and unchained in the small dark room.

Using what light was let in by the small window set high in the wall, she made her way to answer. Her feet were bare, the wooden planks rough to her soles. She'd changed into her dry undies earlier, slipped off her camisole, slipped on one of the clean T-shirts she'd found in Eli's duffel since her blouse was in desperate need of washing.

"Who is it?" she asked, her hands hovering over the locks.

"Elias," he answered, and she wondered why he'd told her, why he'd trusted her to know that his real name was Eli, yet hadn't told her to use the name he went by in the compound.

She released both the locks and stepped back. He walked in, secured the door, crossed to the desk, and struck a match to the wick of the small oil lamp there. It was then that she realized the barracks weren't wired for electricity. She reached for the fan, found it ran on batteries, felt like a twit.

And it was then, too, that he realized she was wearing his shirt and very little else. "Just because we're living together doesn't mean we're sharing community property."

She cast him a withering look that was lost in the dim light of the room. "What did you find out from Rabbit?"

"We're on." Eli lifted his duffel onto the desk, obviously to check the contents for evidence of her pilfering. "The transport will be arriving unexpectedly a day early. We pull this off, and the girls will be out of here tomorrow."

She couldn't believe it. She couldn't speak. She could barely breathe. One day back, and he'd done what she hadn't been able to do in months. If he hadn't been away for so long . . . if he'd been healthy and whole, able to plot and scheme and work his contacts . . .

She sank back onto the bed where she'd been sleeping, overwhelmed with the truth of what she had done. Since discovering the compound's location, she'd watched trucks drop girls at the airport two separate times. Both after she'd sent Eli puking and packing with what had seemed like an oh-so-clever method of getting him out of the way.

She scrubbed both hands down her face, smearing tears she wasn't aware she was crying over cheeks. Eli, of course, chose that minute to glance over; she'd obviously been silent too long.

"Hey, are you okay?" He zipped up his duffel, frowning, tossed it to the floor, and shoved it beneath the second bed. "I thought that would be good news."

"It is." She nodded. "It's great news."

He waved toward her, an offhanded gesture signaling a confused uncertainty. "So, those are what? Happy tears? Or whatever the hell women call it when they cry instead of laugh?"

"Yeah. Happy tears," she lied, by now on the verge of an hysterical sob fest.

She inhaled deeply to settle her nerves—and to suck down the urge to come clean and tell him what she'd done. "It's wonderful, what you've managed. Of course it is, and I'm thrilled. I just hate that so many girls have been lost to their families already."

"Well," he began, sitting on the bed opposite her. "The original plan that brought me here went a lot deeper into the organization running this operation. It's the accelerated timetable screwing us up. We'll get to the core eventually. Right now we'll just deal with the rotten fruit."

"So if you'd been here all this time . . ." God, she couldn't even bring herself to finish the sentence.

He shrugged. "Who knows? We might be exactly where we are now."

"I doubt that," she said with a laugh. "Look what you've done today in less than twelve hours."

He stared at her for several seconds that seemed longer than they were because of the guilt eating her inside. His gaze appeared to be searching, looking beyond what she'd said for the truth she was desperate to hide.

And she was desperate, yes. Desperate to get out of here in one piece. She'd tried to kill him. He could retaliate easily; in a place like this, who would care? Who would know?

When he finally spoke, his voice was low, the tone soothing, the pitch soft. Her insides reacted as if to a seduction. Oh God, but it had been forever since she'd been seduced.

"All I've done here is what I'm trained to do. Don't beat yourself up. You don't have my resources. You did good to get this far."

"Right. I did good to get caught while doing what *I'm* trained to do."

"And I was poisoned," he said, elbows on his knees as he leaned forward, leaned closer. "Someone got to me because I'd let down my guard. I'd let the situation get personal when I should've stayed detached."

"Detached?" Her eyes widened. Incredulity simmered in her blood. "You know what's happening here and you can stay detached?"

"I have to. If I don't"—he rubbed one thumb over the knuckles of his other hand, frowning down at the repetitive motion—"well, you see what happened. I lost my edge. And I need that to stay alive."

She pulled up her feet, tucked them cross-legged beneath her, tugged the hem of his T-shirt down between her thighs when his gaze moved from his hands to drift that direction.

Strangely, having him look at her bothered her not at all. She felt back on even ground, more hopeful than in a very long time. He'd recognized her skills, complimented her as an equal—or close enough to a compliment in her book to count.

And—this was the big one, the one that made him human—he'd admitted that he couldn't stay detached from what was happening here. That the failure to do so, in fact, was the reason they were here, together, in a time and place and situation she would never have imagined could happen.

"Do you face death often? Doing what you do?" she asked softly, wanting to know more about who he was, to dispel her fantasies painting him larger than life.

"More often than is good for me," he said with a hint of a smile.

"But you do it anyway," she responded, curious as to exactly what "it" was that he did.

He breathed deeply, exhaled slowly, as if gearing up or weighing how much he wanted to say, finally saying no more than, "It's in my blood, I guess."

"What? Righting wrongs? Facing danger? Taking risks?"

"A, B, and C."

She shook her head. "Well, you've definitely come to the right place. Though how you managed to discover Ramon's compound when I can't get anyone in law enforcement to even listen when I talk is beyond me."

"I'm not exactly in law enforcement," he admitted, leaning back against the wall, his hands laced and propped on his very flat, very lean, very sexy belly.

Well. This was interesting. She finger-combed her hair away from her forehead. The strands, as straight as they were, fell right back where they'd been. She could see them catch the glow from the lamp, could see that he noticed, too.

Employing her feminine wiles—if she could find them—might actually get her an answer. "If not law enforcement, then what? Freelance of some sort? A mercenary? Black ops?"

He shook his head, grinned a grin that revealed his gorgeous white teeth and her susceptibility to pretty bad boys. "My black ops days are over. What I do now is private sector."

"I've never worked with any P.I. who had the contacts you obviously do. Arranging to hijack the transport on a moment's notice?"

"I'm not a P.I. And hijacking's not quite the right word."

"Fine." And if he wasn't a P.I., what was he? "Commandeering then. Or whatever. And right under Ramon's nose." She scooted back into the center of the bed, shaking her head. "You've got bigger balls than I do."

He laughed then, a sound that was as earthy and raw as it was musical. "I certainly hope so."

She tried out another withering glare but knew she'd have trouble getting it right with the seduction of his laugh tempting parts of her body that hadn't been tempted for a very long time.

"You know what I mean," she finally said. "Taking down his operation while he's looking on. And while working as his right-hand man."

He tilted his head to one side and considered her. "Undercover Work 101. Blend in so that no one has reason to paint a target on your back."

At least no one you know might want to, she mused with no small amount of ill humor. It was the unknown to which his humanity had made him vulnerable. A vulnerability proving that he was a good man. "Well, P.I. Work 101 has me worried that someone somewhere might have a parabolic mic picking up this entire conversation."

He shook his head. "The only electronic equipment in a five-mile radius worth a crap belongs to me."

She wondered if that meant her truck had been discovered and trashed. Her satellite phone, her PDA, her GPS tracking device. Her digital and 35mm cameras, her video cam.

Her gun.

She closed her eyes for a moment, leaned her head back against the wall, counted up all the money she was out, and groaned.

She needed sleep, not a financial analysis. Needed to actually make the bed this time instead of passing out on the bare mattress. But even closing her eyes to gather her bearings left her uneasy with him in the room. She had no idea how she would manage to actually sleep.

She heard the creak of the bedsprings opposite her, looked over to see that Eli had shifted forward again.

"I'll turn down the light," he said. "Let you get back to sleep."

She shook her head, offered a tentative smile. "I'm not really tired. Just thinking."

"About?"

Was he really curious or only making small talk? "About surrendering my license and taking up stripping for a living."

She'd been trying to lighten the moment, to make him laugh so she could savor more of the sound. But what happened was that he stayed silent, his gaze traveling over her in a slow burning crawl.

He started with her bare feet and legs; she'd stretched them out earlier when leaning back on the wall. Her hands rested on the bed at her hips, and she refused to draw attention to the hem of the T-shirt by tugging it down.

Her thong wasn't visible, but the entire length of her legs was in view, and he noticed. Tugging on the T-shirt would also plaster the olive green cotton flat to her breasts, and she was more than well aware that movement of any sort made clear her lack of a bra.

When he reached her neck, however, was when she discovered his fetish. He took his time lingering there, enough time that she felt her nipples begin to harden. It was all she could do not to reach for the rough blanket and pull it up to her chin.

She felt the touch of his gaze along the column of her throat, felt it as he took his time at the base in the hollow where her pulse thumped madly. And it wasn't until he'd set her skin ablaze that he finally looked into her eyes.

"Thank you for what you did this evening."

She wanted to be quick-witted and clever, to prove she had as much brain to offer as body, but the only words that came to her to say were, "You're welcome."

After a moment he nodded, and then he slowly got to his feet. His gaze drifted to the floor. One brow lifted ominously. "You know I'm going to have to lock you up again before we go to bed."

"What?" Her pulse jumped to a brand new beat. "Why?"

His mouth twisted into a wry grin. "Let's just call it a matter of trust."

"More like a matter of distrust," she grumbled, scooting to the edge of the bed and dangling one leg over.

"Semantics," he said, crouching down to lock her up, his fingers lingering where they cupped the sole of her foot once he'd secured her ankle. "Right now, the only person I know I can trust is Rabbit."

"Fine." She jerked free from his grasp, the chain clinking as she settled her foot on the bed. "The only person I can trust is myself."

"Then we'll have to work on trusting each other, won't we?" he asked, stripping off his shirt and turning back to the second bed. "In the meantime I suggest we both get some sleep. If all hell breaks loose tomorrow, we'll need the clear heads."

She didn't respond except to close her eyes and settle in beneath the blanket. Thinking of tomorrow left her restless, so she thought about Eli's bare chest instead—a mistake of a different color.

He'd been breathing deeply for hours before she managed to sleep.

Eight

Eli didn't think Stella would ever go to sleep. He lay for hours unmoving, breathing in a slow, steady, regulated rhythm that he knew had convinced her he'd long since passed out. He hadn't, of course.

He was simply an expert at playing dead.

He'd done it in Bosnia, in Afghanistan, in Lebanon. His SG-5 partners accused him of learning to breathe through his pores. They'd searched him for gills, refusing to believe any human being could breathe without detection. He'd learned. He'd had to.

He'd have been dead a long time ago had he not.

His chaining her hadn't been about trust as much as about keeping her safe. Were she to get a burr up her butt and sneak out while he slept, he wouldn't do her much good as protection. He could name one or two of Ramon's men who wouldn't hesitate to bind, gag, and rape her no matter that Aceveda wanted her undamaged and clean.

Only Ramon understood who all of them here actually worked for, and even then he didn't have full knowledge of Spectra IT's far-reaching scope. Most of the men here were no better than scum.

Unemployable, unsavory, untrustworthy, unkind.

Putting Stella out there had been a huge risk. Keeping her close now was paramount.

Now that her breathing had settled and he knew that she slept, he did what any good voyeur would do—rolled onto his side and turned up the flame on the oil lamp. Sitting and talking with her earlier had been a hard won test of self-control. His newly reclaimed self-control—one it had taken four solid months of recuperation to find.

He hadn't exactly been the most congenial houseguest to ever stay on Hank's farm.

He'd always known and accepted that life was a series of trials, some won, others lost, and presented in a variety of colors, shapes, and sizes. Between them, the men of the Smithson Group had suffered the gamut. With Hank's help and a lot from one another, each had always pulled through.

But he had to say that this last go-round had been close to the worst he had known.

Stella stirred, kicked the blanket from her shackled foot. The chain rattled and she opened her eyes, grimacing, yet not awake or focused enough to realize he was watching.

Knowing firsthand the heavy, sweaty discomfort of leg irons . . . he winced in empathy. He could let her loose, and lose the rest of the night's sleep he needed. Or let her loose and sleep with her.

Oh, yeah. He was an expert who knew all about staying detached, didn't he?

"If you're going to stay awake and stare, would you at least take this thing off my leg so one of us can get some sleep?"

He slid his gaze from her foot to her face. "No can do. I need at least two or three hours of sound shut-eye, and can't get it unless I know that you're safe."

"I thought this was about trust, not safety," she said after a thick silence that went on two heartbeats too long.

The two became three, then four, then five before his admission of the truth burst free. "I lied."

"Lied? About not trusting me?"

"No. The trust we still have to work on," he said.

She pushed up onto her elbows. "Then what's this crap about my safety?"

"It's not crap. I want you safe."

"Right. To hand over to the big guy."

"That's bullshit, and you know it."

"Do I? Sure seems to be the rumor in the air." She jerked her foot and the chain. "And this doesn't help dispel it."

"It's Ramon's men who pose the real threat. Not Aceveda. By the time he arrives, we'll be gone." He was not about to tell her that he refused to fail her the way he'd failed so many of the girls.

He hadn't protected them. He hadn't kept them safe.

She could think what she wanted; the truth was his own hell to pay.

"Just go back to sleep," he finally ordered, his thoughts echoing off the four walls of the very small room.

"What about you?" she asked, her tone gentle and low.

He felt her voice the way he wanted to feel the strands of her hair. A soft silky tease brushing over his senses. "Yeah. Me, too."

"Except you haven't been asleep yet at all, have you?"

He swung his legs over the side of the bed to sit, curling his hands into the thin edge of the mattress. He glared at her as he said, "I haven't, no. And it looks like I'm not going to since you won't shut up."

"Are you a heavy sleeper?"

He shook his head.

"Do you toss and turn?"

"No one's mentioned it lately."

She smiled at that, a smile that spoke volumes without a single, explanatory word. He thought about dousing the light and falling back onto his brick of a pillow. He thought about grabbing his rifle from beneath his bed and heading out the door.

But he thought the longest and the hardest about what her smile meant, what she would do if he turned her loose and crawled into her bed. If either of them would sleep. If either of them would want to.

"Okay," she finally said. "Here's the thing. We both need sleep. Neither one of us are getting any like this. The way I see it, you let me go and then we have three options."

Funny how her count matched his. "And those are?"

"One, we push the beds together. Two, we upend the frames and make a full mattress on the floor. Or, three. We sleep back-to-back on whichever bed is most comfortable."

He voted for door number three minus the back-to-back part. "We start moving furniture, we wake up everyone in the barracks."

"Not to mention I could still climb off my half without you knowing."

A zero percent possibility, but still. "There is that."

"Then it's settled." She stuck out her foot, offering access to the lock. "You pick the bed. Or, better yet. Stack the two mattresses on the one frame. Who knows? The extra thickness might even cushion the bulge of the springs."

That wasn't the bulge that concerned him. "And if it doesn't?"

Her grin was like a sickle swathing a path through his gut. "Then I'll wake up bruised and battered, like the princess who slept on the very small pea."

Now she really couldn't sleep. There were bulges every-where. Shoulders, biceps, buttocks, calves. He was lean but he was large, and he took up a whole hell of a lot of her bed.

She wanted to roll over onto her back. She wanted to punch a pillow beneath her. She wanted to pull up her knees into a fetal position, but she didn't have room.

This had been such a bad idea.

God, what was she saying? Everything she'd done for the last six months had been questionable; she was just realizing the extent of it now—now that she was sleeping with the very same man she'd tried to kill.

No. She hadn't wanted him dead, only out of the way. Or so it was easy to convince herself now that she knew him and realized he shared her goal of ridding the world of this compound.

If they got out in one piece, she'd tell him all of the truth, the full story of what had gone down. She just wouldn't tell him before. She'd confess what she'd done, explain the whys, the wherefores, and apologize.

And that would be that. They'd go their separate ways. No hard feelings. Everything all good.

And tomorrow morning she'd wake up on a beach in Tahiti. Like blowing out the candles on a birthday cake. Wish it hard enough and, poof! It came true.

"This was your idea, you know. If you can't get to sleep, don't blame me."

She held her breath and didn't move, waiting for the rumble of Eli's voice to quiet, for the vibration thrumming beneath the surface of her skin to settle before she spoke. "I wasn't blaming you for anything. I was just worried I'd wake you up if I turned over."

"Turn away. I doubt I'm going to get any sleep."

Like she'd said. A bad idea. "Do you want to switch back to the other bed?"

"Do you want to spend the night in leg irons?"

What she wanted was sleep. She was tired and keyed up and unable to find any semblance of balance with his bulk at her back, his heat warming her, though their blankets kept their skin from touching. Eli was fully dressed anyway. He'd taken off only his boots.

She sighed. "I'd like it better if you used silk scarves."

He didn't say a word, didn't respond by moving, by

breathing harder, by shifting position to move farther away. It was as if he hadn't heard her at all, or was ignoring what she'd said.

So she went ahead and dug her grave deeper. "I just meant the metal's pretty heavy and tight and makes my ankle sweat, and I was thinking a fabric bond would be easier to sleep in."

Yeah. Of course she was. Sleeping was the only thing on her mind. She wasn't wondering a bit how his skin would feel without fatigues and blankets between them.

She wasn't the least bit curious about his hair's texture, whether it grew thick or sparse on his chest, how it grew elsewhere.

And she had no desire to know how he kissed, if he teased or demanded or tempted or took. All she wanted was sleep.

Behind her, Eli rolled onto his back. "What about my T-shirt? The one you're wearing?"

Her heart thudded. "What about it?"

"If you take it off, I'll rip it into strips and use them to tie you up."

"You want to tie me up?"

"Didn't we have this discussion earlier?"

"That was about trust and safety."

"And this is?"

She took a deep breath. "Bondage?"

He turned again, onto his side; she felt him spoon in behind her, felt him fight with the blankets until they shared only one, until it was the fabric of his fatigues and not the blanket scratching the backs of her thighs.

She tried not to shiver, but then his hand settled into the dip in her hip and he spread his fingers. His touch spanned the width of her leg.

"No, Stella," he said, his words whispering through the hair at the back of her neck. "Bondage is consensual."

God, what was he saying? What was he doing? "I didn't fight you, did I?"

"No, but you didn't want it."

Oh, he was so very wrong. "So now you're an expert on bondage?"

His hand on her hip moved higher, settling over the elastic of her thong. "Don't ask me that unless you really want me to answer."

Was that what she wanted? For him to show her what he would do to a woman he'd tied down? "Answer, then. I want to know."

"You want me to tell you?" His voice was gruff . . . then grew more so. "Or do you want me to show you?"

"What do you want?" She was already chest-deep in danger. Tossing away the rest of her caution hardly seemed reckless. "You decide."

He laughed then, a low, growling, roll-of-thunder rumble that came up from his gut. "What if I decide we both need sleep more than a lesson in bondage?"

Could the "L" on her loser forehead be any larger? She shrugged. "Sure, whatever."

Again with the laugh. And now with the hand creeping beneath the T-shirt to rest in the curve of her waist. She shivered, drew up her knees.

He cuddled up tighter into her body, pulling her back into his. "Then it's settled. We sleep."

It didn't matter that he was right, that they had no business taking off their clothes, that they needed sleep for tomorrow. She still felt like the only girl without a Friday night date.

Boys don't make passes at girls who wear glasses. Neither did they want a woman in a battered straw hat and blue jeans who was licensed to carry a gun and knew more about using it than about baking cakes.

Still, her pulse settled quickly, as did her nerves. The beat of his heart against her back, his palm on her belly, his breath in her hair . . . she found herself lulled into a state of restfulness more peaceful than she'd known in weeks—months, if truth be told.

As if she'd been waiting for this man to calm her. This man whose last name she didn't even know.

He relaxed remarkably fast as well, as if by some strange chance, some very long shot, he needed her, too.

Nine

Amazingly enough, they'd both slept. He didn't realize that he'd done so until he came awake sometime before dawn. His history of sleeping with women was about notching his bedpost—not about actually falling asleep.

He and Stella had both done so, so soundly that neither had woke when they'd tangled together in limbs and bedclothes. And now he found himself scooted to the foot of the bed while she had shifted up the other direction.

This put his face—since she was flat on her back and he lay turned toward her—on her chest, his nose pressed to her breast, his mouth near enough to her nipple that a flick of his tongue and he'd taste her. Taste the T-shirt she wore anyway, and that was close enough.

It was early morning, and he was a man, and whatever they'd offered one another last night—solace or comfort or a sense of all being safe—no longer mattered. All that mattered was this hazy, dreamlike state and her body.

He wanted sex and he wanted it from her.

He spread his hand over her belly, fanning out his fingers so that his thumb brushed the lower curve of one breast, his little finger the edge of her panties. Considering her panties were no more than a fabric scrap held on by elastic, he was pretty damn close to touching her.

She stirred slightly, stretching her arms overhead and moving her body toward him as if seeking more of his touch. Imagined or real, he took her up on the offer, cupping her far breast beneath the T-shirt, nuzzling his face into the near one, deciding as much as he liked her wearing his things, the shirt had to go.

He raised up onto one elbow and leaned over, dislodging the blanket. The faint light filtering through the window above the bed barely allowed him to see. Feeling was another thing entirely, and he was able to learn all about her with the touch of his hands, pushing the hem of the shirt to her neck, angling over her, tucking into her cleavage, breathing her in.

She groaned softly, one hand coming down to cup the back of his head, her back arching up instinctively. He liked her reaction, liked it a lot, and tilted his hips more toward her, wedging one knee between hers. She spread her legs accordingly, but he waited.

He wasn't yet sure how much of this she thought she was dreaming, and he wanted her fully awake. He wanted her permission less than he wanted her participation. But he wouldn't take her without having both, no matter the maddening insistence of his hard-on.

He nuzzled the skin of her belly, kissed her abdomen, stroked his hand the length of her thigh. When she finally woke, she stilled and stiffened and forgot for a long time to breathe. He knew that because by then he'd rested his head on her bare chest and she wasn't moving.

And so he kissed her, a very soft, very subtle brush of his lips to her sternum. Against one cheek, beneath one palm, her nipples hardened. He grinned to himself and kissed her again, this time opening his mouth, cupping her close, and sucking lightly at her sweetly plump flesh.

She arched her back, lifted her hips, threaded her fingers

into his hair, and held tight. He took that as a sign and moved his mouth to the center of her breast, tugging at her nipple, which felt like a gumdrop on his tongue.

She whimpered as he sucked, her hand falling from his head to his shoulder. She kneaded the muscle there, matching the rhythm of his mouth, hooking her heel behind his thigh and urging him close.

Permission, participation, and a promise of pleasure. He pushed up to his knees and crawled on top, cupping the full weight of her breasts and crushing them together, licking his way from one peak to the other.

His balls tingled, and his cock thickened inside his shorts. He wanted to fuck her, to come until he turned inside out. But that was his dick talking. The rest of him wanted the door locked and the lights on so he could see her sweat. Because he knew she'd be the type to do so.

He began kissing his way down her belly then; she stopped him, shoving him up and away. Straddling her, he sat kneeling, leaning back on his heels. She didn't say a word. All she did was work her way out of the shirt and toss it to the floor. She tossed the pillow, too.

He still didn't move, waiting to see what she wanted. Getting his would be easy; she was gorgeous and he was hard. But he wanted this for her. Because of what she'd been through. What she'd done for him. In case today went down in the very bad way he feared might occur.

He couldn't see her eyes except to know they were open. He could barely see her body but for the contrast between blanket and skin. He didn't need to see anything. He felt her touch, her fingertips like matchsticks on his skin, there above his waistband, burning him up.

She moved higher, exploring the hair on his belly, his abs, ribs, and pecs. When she gripped his biceps and pulled him down, he fell forward, bracing his weight above her, his hands on the bed at her sides.

She continued to play, and he let her, let her until he

ground his jaw into dust, until he could feel the teeth of his zipper biting into his cock.

And that was it. Either he got his or gave her hers. Waiting would take a stronger man than he was.

He scooted down her legs until he sat between her ankles and knees, and bent to taste her belly. She squirmed, her hands clutching the edges of the mattress when he dipped his tongue into her navel, slipped his fingers beneath the fabric scrap of her thong. She was wet already. Moisture seeped from between her pussy's bare lips; he spread it like thick honey over the plumped up flesh of her sex.

He'd planned to take things slowly, to tease her until she couldn't take it anymore, but she was already wet and ready and he couldn't wait. Sucking her into his mouth and tasting her juice was the only thing he wanted.

Her thong was useless as a barrier. He settled his mouth over the thin gauzy fabric and used it ruthlessly in his quest to bring her off. He drew her clit between his lips and sucked, holding tight to the hard knot and swirling his tongue around it. The fabric felt like a cat's tongue to his lips, wet and rough and warm.

Whatever she felt, the sensation was fierce enough that she caught back a cry and fought to free her feet from beneath him. He lifted up and let her go. Knees raised, she pulled her heels to her hips, and opened her legs wide. He slipped his palms down the inside of her thighs until his thumbs met between.

Her skin was so soft, and she smelled wonderfully female, salty and marine, like she'd washed with soap and sea water. He pulled her panties out of the way, nuzzled his nose to the crease between her leg and her sex, and breathed deeply of her moistness and musk.

She was shivering, and breathing wasn't enough for either of them. He wanted more of her taste, and took it, pushing his tongue inside of her, pulling out to eat at the folds he held open, spearing her again, in and out, his thumb circling her clit all the while.

She arched up into his mouth, and he replaced his tongue with two fingers, fucking her with them while he tongued and sucked at the hard bud of nerves where her sensation was centered.

She flung a forearm over her mouth as she came, shuddering beneath him, muffling the sounds she made. He wanted to hear her. He wanted to be anywhere else but where they were so he could hear her. So they could explore each other on cool clean sheets in a room that didn't smell like stale armpits.

But being here with her was better than being alone or being without her, without Stella, and so he brought her down slowly, finishing her with gentle strokes of his tongue and his fingers.

Rather than calming her, however, his touch kept her on edge, kept her body wired and tense. She was tight, her muscles clenched, her breathing ragged. She sat up so quickly she forced him to scramble back. He nearly fell to the floor.

And then she ordered him, "Take off your pants," while slipping out of her thong and turning over onto her knees.

Presented with any woman's naked ass—but this one especially—along with a harsh demand to strip, he was hardly going to argue. In fact, he was off the bed and out of his skivvies in less time than it took her to punch up the pillow and tuck it beneath her chest.

He climbed back onto the bed behind her, fitting his body to hers, his cock seeking the warmth there between her thighs and higher, where she was still wet and still ready, begging him by doing no more than wiggling close.

He didn't even hesitate, seeking her entrance with the head of his cock and sliding inside. She gasped as he hit bottom, gasped then groaned and pushed against him, seeking more. He settled his hands at her hips and held tight.

And then he began to move, his strokes starting out long but rapidly growing hard and impatient. As ready as he was to come, he wanted her to want this even more.

He grit his teeth and set a rhythm that had her crying out into the mattress where she'd buried her face. The sounds she made were wild, echoing through the bed frame, vibrating into his bones.

He reached around to massage her clit and she came again just like that, shuddering around him, milking him, squeezing him until he was done for, his control snapped.

With one sharp cry, he let go, thrusting roughly and spilling himself, pounding, pounding, *pounding*, fingers bruising her hips, his head swimming.

And then he was empty. He was spent. He pulled himself free . . . yet she still wanted more.

She pushed up to her knees, and this time told him, "Lie down. On your back. Hurry."

He did, not about to deny her a thing, wondering, though, where her desperation came from, what she was looking for, what she thought he could give her when she didn't know him at all. She seemed frantic, needy, savage in a way that brought to mind making penance; he wondered only briefly who it was she owed and what he had to do with her debt.

He wondered only briefly because once he was on his back, she knelt between his legs. He'd barely begun to soften when she started kissing him. His thighs, his belly. She twined her fingers into the line of hair thick beneath his navel and held him like she thought he might leave the bed.

He wanted to soothe her. He did, in fact, reach down to stroke her hair. But then she took him into her mouth, closing her lips around the base of his shaft, using her tongue on the underside as she sucked her way back to the head. He reached for the pillow, pressed it flat to his face, and spread his legs wider.

His eyes rolled back, his stomach clenched. He shouldn't be able to do this so soon and already, but his body had never known the persistence of Stella Banks. She swirled her tongue around his ridge, swept it across the flat of his head, teased it down the seam underneath. He flexed his ass and prayed his balls had her staying power.

It was wild, the way she sucked him off, her hair dangling and teasing his legs, her fingers exploring deep between his cheeks, finding erogenous zones no woman before had cared to discover.

This one was fearless and ruthless, and he swore he was going to die. He had hockey pucks for balls, a dick like a wooden bat, and her mouth sliding up and down him like his very own hand. It felt like being sucked off and jerked off all at the same time.

And then she quit. And he groaned. But only halfheartedly, because a second later she was climbing up to straddle him. His cock in her hand, she held him in position and took him inside, lowering herself until she sat flush against him.

She braced her hands on his chest. He ringed her wrists with his fingers. And she began to ride, slowly, grinding against him. Her clit was hard where it rubbed the base of his cock. With her head tossed back, her hair hanging to her waist, dawn's first light shining through the window and lighting her skin, she looked like a goddess, or a painting, or some otherworldly being.

For a long moment he wasn't sure he could breathe. All he could do was stare up at her and watch the movement of her body, the expression on her face, the tilt of her head, the flare of her nostrils, the tip of her tongue caught between her lips.

This time she stopped fighting for silence. Her breathing echoed audibly. A raspy groan filtered up her throat, and she sat straighter, sliding her palms up her thighs, her torso, cupping her breasts.

She squeezed, and tweaked at her nipples, then leaned back, settling one palm on his thigh behind her and bracing her weight. The sensation of her movements, the slide of her pussy over his cock . . . his entire body was ready to snap.

And she continued to make it worse, reaching between his legs with her free hand, fondling his balls, fingering his ass, playing until he was wound tight enough to lose consciousness, and his eyes rolled back in his head.

Enough! *Enough*!

He growled, pushed himself up to sit facing her, and grabbed both of her hands. He wrapped her arms around his neck, wrapped his around her waist, nuzzled his lips to her throat.

She squirmed, but held on. "You tickle."

"My mouth?" he murmured.

"Your mouth. The hair on your chest." She squirmed again. "You're yummy."

He chuckled. "Yummy?"

She nodded. "Oh yeah."

He knew what he wanted. Right then, with her wiggling against him, tightening around his throbbing cock, rubbing her nipples against his chest, he knew what he wanted more than he wanted to come.

He splayed one hand in the center of her back, slid up the other to cup her head, pulled her toward him, and kissed her.

She stiffened briefly, and he wondered what she had against his kiss, if the contact of his mouth to hers ruined her fantasy of indulging in pleasure without intimacy.

Because that was the sense he had, that she wanted a separation of body and mind.

Tough shit. She wasn't getting it.

He ground his mouth harder, and felt resistance seep from her body immediately. Her lips parted and she became the aggressor. It was her tongue boldly seeking his own.

And then just as suddenly she gentled the kiss, whimpering softly as if injured or hurt or caught in a trap that would kill her. He crushed her body against him, holding her, reassuring her, keeping her safe.

She broke away then and began to move, rotating her hips in a slow, sexy belly dance. The rhythm nearly shorted out his self-control. He lowered his weight onto his elbows, let his head fall back, and closed his eyes.

She worked her magic on his body, riding him so sweetly that sex before Stella ceased to exist. The fingers of both her hands dug into his thighs to hold on, and she used the leverage to slide up and down, stroking him, squeezing him . . . it was what he needed. It was perfect, and his staying power was shot.

He came, a burst of sensation straight from his gut. His balls ached, and he surged upward, shuddering until he was empty, thinking he would never again catch his breath or know the normal beat of his heart.

And then, as if she'd been waiting for him to be done, she finished. Her spasms gripped his cock as she rubbed against him, grinding her clit to bring herself off. She was gorgeous. She was wild. And for some goddamn reason, she had to be in control.

He'd never known another woman like her. He doubted another existed. And for one brief moment he wished their circumstances weren't so fucked up, because he wanted to know her more.

Ten

When Stella woke a second time and fully, it was to the sound of a diesel engine, one uncommon to the compound and meaning only one thing.

The transport was here.

If Eli's friends pulled this off, the girls would be on their way home and the compound reduced to rubble by the end of the day.

She tossed back the blanket, swung her legs over the side of the bed, groaned at the stretch and pull of overused muscles, and scrambled for her clothes.

The thong she'd washed while she'd showered had dried during the night, draped from the desk along with her camisole. She pulled on both items, putting her missing thong and just how she'd lost it from her mind as she tugged on socks then jeans then her plain oxford shirt.

What had happened earlier in this room would stay in this room, the memory one best left behind, since she would have no cause ever to see Eli again. She had her life, he had his. And their two worlds had no reason ever to collide again—even if she wished like hell that they did.

Besides, there was that thing about the way men tired so

quickly of the brash and mouthy attitude that came with the long legs and blond hair.

And then there was that other thing about her trying to kill him.

Ignoring a pang of . . . she didn't know what it was, didn't *want* to know what it was, didn't want to feel anything for him beyond gratitude that he'd done what she'd been unable to do in freeing the girls . . . ignoring all of that, she sat on the edge of the bed to pull on her boots.

The scent of sex rose to remind her of lying naked with him earlier. She ignored that, too. She didn't need the reminder right now, could've done without it quite nicely, in fact. At least until she was home and could deal with the stupid choices she'd made yet again at a time when she couldn't afford to be so incredibly dumb.

What was it with her and getting involved with all the wrong men?

Boots on, she dug in her bag for her hairbrush, smoothed her hair quickly, twisted it into a knot, and secured it on the back of her head with the pencil she'd found in a drawer of the desk.

Leaving her shirt hanging loose to shield her body, she jammed her hat on her head, brim tugged over her eyes, and opened the door. Rabbit leaned against the wall beside it, chewing on a piece of straw.

Stella rolled her eyes. "Don't tell me I'm stuck in here all day."

He pushed off the wall and shrugged. "Not really, but if you want out, you are stuck with me."

She considered him briefly. Tall and built. Gorgeous flat stomach, toned shoulders. Great silvery gray eyes. Dark hair curling over his nape . . . and he did nothing for her the way Eli did.

The way Eli had for months.

The way thinking of him did even now, damn her weakness for sexy, intelligent, principled men who could take what she dished and serve it right back.

She smiled, but the thought gave her way too much pause and she pushed it away. "Why do they call you Rabbit?"

He shook his head. "You don't want to know."

"What's your given name?"

"Harry."

She nodded thoughtfully, shook off the personal and got back to business where she belonged. "That was the transport I heard, wasn't it? It's here, right?"

"Sounded like it."

"God, I can't believe this has all happened so fast." She stepped out, pulled the door shut behind her. "Can we go?"

"You stick close. We hang back and don't get involved with any of what's going on." Harry stepped onto the bottom stair, flicked the straw onto the ground. "And we don't cause a stir. If the men start messing with you, it's back to being locked up. Eli said so."

"Yeah, well, Eli doesn't run the world," she grumbled, hurrying down the porch steps, her pounding steps unable to beat down the thrill at knowing that he thought of her and wanted her safe.

"In this case, he does," Harry said, moving up to her side. "The transport should be in position to load. We watch from the porch in front of Ramon's office."

"Fine." She didn't care if her ticket matched a seat in the nosebleed section as long as she got to see the girls go free. And as long as Eli was in the picture.

But she did slow down and walk a step behind Harry, her hands in her pockets, her head lowered. She wasn't about to make eye contact with anyone—especially Eli—and raise undue suspicion.

She and Harry rounded the end of the long row of barracks, keeping close to the cluster of buildings as they headed for the office. Once around the corner, the cages came into view. The transport trailer was indeed backed up to the gate.

Only it wasn't loading. The girls huddled in the doorway of their tar paper shelter while a group of men stood together at the front of the truck. Their voices were raised; heated words carried across the compound yard. Their stance, as a group, was confrontational. Aggressive, even. And dangerous.

She followed Harry up the steps, doing her best to act as his docile prisoner while sizing up the activity a hundred feet away. She recognized Eli, Ramon, Arturo, and two of the other men. Then there were the three she'd never before seen. Eli's friends, she was certain.

And they were in Eli's face, Ramon's and Arturo's, too, giving as good as they got from the compound staff.

Whatever was going on here, it was not good, and a frisson of fear shot through her.

She glanced covertly at Harry, hoping for a signal or a sense of his reaction, wondering if he was worried, if she should be, too, but his expression was the perfect undercover blank slate and was absolutely no use in helping her determine how royally things were screwed.

She returned her attention to the three men dressed similarly to Eli and the others, looking as worn and weary yet mercenarily fierce in the drab olive and black as any of Ramon's underlings. Point for the good guys; they knew how to blend in.

The one nearest Eli wore his dark hair shoulder length. He was tall, his eyes hidden behind reflective lenses, his body lean and hard. The man at his side was larger, not in height so much as in bulk. This one's hair was thick and black, his eyes, even from this distance, appearing to reflect the blue of the sky. The third man stood turned to the side, a tribal tattoo at his nape, a bandanna tied around his shaved head. He wore dark glasses and a goatee, and Stella couldn't help but shiver.

As a group, the three were formidable. Add Eli as a fourth, Harry as a fifth, and the testosterone had her shaking in her boots—or would have had the five not been on her side. She didn't doubt for a minute that she and the girls would be clear of here by nightfall. That Ramon and his band of merry goons would pose no threat again.

In the blink of an eye, however, her certainty vanished. Anxiety rolled through her in a nauseating flutter as Ramon held out both hands, waved off the other men with a sharp barking burst of orders. Eli even readied his rifle.

"What's going on?" she whispered, stepping closer to where Harry stood with his shoulder braced on the porch's corner support. As they looked on, Ramon turned with a final halting hand gesture, cutting off whatever it was the others were saying, and headed back in the direction of the office.

"Not sure, but it doesn't look good for the home team."

That much was obvious, what with the three gathering at the cab of the truck and Eli backing away to follow Ramon. She heard him issuing orders to Arturo and the others, heard the name Aceveda.

"He's not going to let them go until after Aceveda gets here," she said to herself more than to Harry. "But won't Aceveda know your guys aren't Ramon's men?"

"No more than Ramon will know they're not Aceveda's. As long as the two don't compare notes, we'll make this work."

"And if they do?"

"Then our window's a whole lot smaller." Harry dropped his voice as the men drew near, and Stella remained silent as the first of the boot steps came down heavily on the porch.

"Señorita Banks," Ramon said, his gaze falling her way. He headed toward her. "In order to secure your safety, Elias will return you to your cage. I can spare no men today to act as your personal bodyguards."

She nodded as meekly as she could manage and lowered her gaze. As much as she wanted visual assurance from Eli that this was one battle lost in a much larger war, Harry's words kept her from seeking it.

Besides, soon enough she would be put on the block to make retribution for what she had done. Until then, she had to focus on staying alive.

Following his meeting with Ramon, Eli left the office to carry out his orders and issue the compound director's directives to the men. First, however, he stopped on the porch and glanced toward the cages housing the girls and Stella.

The transport truck and trailer remained parked in position to load. The fact that Ramon had not ordered Julian, K.J., and Mick to move the rig worked in the Smithson Group's favor. Their objective hadn't changed—only the obstacles.

Ramon's current quest to ready the compound for Aceveda's inspection was another boon Eli wasn't about to overlook. The activity inside the fence made for great cover.

Now all he had to do was run his plan by the others, work out the flaws, and implement stage one tonight in the machine shop with Rabbit. What better way to mask the roar of one diesel engine than with that of another?

He caught movement as Stella stepped out from under the overhang of her shelter. She'd lost the hat, but otherwise remained dressed as she'd been when Arturo escorted her down to the cage.

As she had been when Eli had first seen her this morning after leaving her naked in bed.

A part of him was still reeling from the sex they'd shared. He'd gone into it needing relief from the tension of the day before and the ones still to come. That was all.

But when he'd left the barracks room at dawn, glancing back once to where Stella lay uncovered, he'd realized that one tension had been replaced by another. That what he needed now after having her wasn't going to be satisfied as simply next time.

And that right now what he needed was to make certain she was okay, that she understood he had no intention of abandoning her or sacrificing her or leaving her behind. That he hadn't sloughed off what they'd done as nothing. That his belly was burning with all the ways he wanted her close.

He stepped off the porch, his rifle bumping his hip, and headed for her cage. She saw him coming and stayed where she was rather than meeting him at the gate. She was scared or nervous, less sure of where things stood—of where she stood—now that she'd been caged.

He gestured her closer, wanting to wrap her up in his arms but keeping enough distance between them that no one watching would find their interaction suspicious. He pitched his voice low when he spoke. "You okay?"

"For a rat in a cage?" She nodded, curled her fingers into the chain links until the fence shook with her tension. "I could use a hamster wheel. Run myself into exhaustion so the waiting and wondering doesn't kill me."

He studied her face, the lines of worry bracketing her mouth that he hadn't noticed last night. The circles beneath her eyes that had darkened. He wondered if he'd added to the stress she suffered, and his gut seized up at the thought.

"You're going to be fine."

She barked out a laugh. "Easy for you to say. You're not doing harem prep."

He couldn't help but grin. "Is that what this is?"

She shrugged, glanced away to the main cluster of buildings. The sun shone along individual strands of her hair where they'd escaped the pencil that was somehow holding the rest in a twist on the back of her head.

She was gorgeous and she was hurting and she was putting up a front like he'd never known a woman to do.

He wondered if she'd be just as tough on the outside, and suddenly couldn't wait to know.

"It's pretty close, I guess," she said. "Keeping me pure and untouched while waiting for my master's arrival. I suppose the silk, oil, and incense will be delivered soon enough."

Still she made jokes. And still he stayed where he was, when he wanted more than anything to cover her fingers with his where she held onto the fence like a lifeline.

He looked down at the ground, his sunglasses darkening the dirt to a shadow. His position felt untenable. Caught, as he was, between his loyalty to SG-5 and the very woman he'd arrived yesterday determined to remove from his mission's equation.

Now he was charged with removing her as he would an artifact—one needing to be kept under wraps, secretly smuggled from beneath the nose of security. It wasn't a situation with which Eli was unfamiliar, just one he worked like hell to avoid tangling with.

He glanced back up, moved a step closer, spoke in a voice that was almost a whisper because it had to be said. If not, it would hover between them like Damocles's Sword, and they were already facing too much danger. "You're not exactly untouched."

She snorted. "Yeah, well, you would know."

He never knew what to expect from her. Never. But he did recognize battle armor when he saw it. "I do know, Stella. And I enjoyed touching you a hell of a lot."

"Why? Because you got to me before Aceveda?"

He bit off a string of sharp curses, but not before her chin came up and her gaze demanded he explain the foul-mouthed and uncharacteristic outburst. It wasn't like he owned her, she seemed to be saying. And he sure hadn't staked a claim.

Or had he?

The thought nearly choked him. "No. Because I enjoyed

touching you. Because you responded in a way that I took to mean you got off to it, too."

"Several times, as a matter of fact," she said, brow raised. "But then you know that, don't you?"

He didn't know he could drop his voice any lower, but he did, and found himself practically hissing. "Does that bother you? Me bringing you off so easily? You'd rather it be Aceveda?"

"I'd rather it be no one," she spat out. "No one. Do you understand?"

What he saw in her eyes then was fear. Fear of the sort he hadn't seen when she'd learned of her fate as a prize in a game of roulette, or when she'd taken off her clothes for Ramon's goons, even when she'd been sentenced back to her cage.

It was a fear he didn't understand, but which he was certain was a fear for her emotional life. He had no idea where it came from, but wrapping his mind around the reality didn't take a rocket scientist. Not after the way she'd given herself to him.

"We're going to get out of here, Stella. All of us. I'm not leaving anyone behind."

"You'd better leave Ramon, or forget it. The deal's off," she grumbled sarcastically, her chin down, a tiny grin teasing her lips.

He sighed because otherwise he would laugh. "You stay awake tonight, okay? You pay attention to any sound you hear."

She narrowed her gaze and looked at him sideways. "Aren't you undercover types supposed to be quiet?"

"Only when we're not purposefully causing distractions," he said.

"Right." She nodded, shading her eyes. "I'll listen for the distraction."

He was done playing or flirting or whatever it was they

were doing here to avoid talking about the way she'd mounted him and begged. "Ramon has everyone in the compound working all night. There's going to be a lot going on, but my guys are looking to move the transport close to dawn."

He needed her to be ready. Needed her to get that this was real and it was going down and he'd protect her but she had to protect herself.

"Got it," she said.

"I need you to get it, Stella. I need you to be ready."

She turned to him then; her armor of sarcasm and insincerity falling away. "I'll be ready, Eli. I'll be ready."

Eleven

She remained ready for the fifteen hours that followed, hunkered down beneath the overhang of her shelter, her hat pulled low on her face, watching the hustle in the compound that made her think of New York City without the lights and the glitz and the crowds.

She'd always wanted to go to New York City, had never taken the time, the chance, the opportunity. She preferred the familiar streets of Del Rio, those of Ciudad Acuña. In either she could lose herself, hide in the shadows of doorways, lurk in alleys, and stay safe at all times by controlling her risk.

It was when she put too much trust in others, when she loosened her hold, tempted the unknown . . . those were the times she got hurt. And she feared knowing Eli would mean she'd get hurt.

Not because of what he'd do when he discovered her role in his poisoning—role, hell. Her responsibility *for* his poisoning. But because of the way he'd looked into her eyes while they'd made love. That was the sort of hurt she avoided, the sort of hurt she feared.

And he *had* made love to her, not simply taken her the way she'd wanted. He'd seen to her needs, assured himself he left her well-pleased, before he considered himself. She hadn't wanted it that way. She'd tried to keep what they'd done about sex. Why he had to let it get complicated and messy was beyond her to comprehend. Men weren't usually like that.

Men simply took what they wanted, and she'd learned not to expect anything more. Now, however, wasn't the time to get maudlin over the way men made her moody. Right now was all about what was happening in the cage next to hers.

Large male bodies lurked in the shadows thrown by the bulk of the transport. The moon, no more than a fingernail, barely hung onto the horizon. She could see movement, but little more, and would think it all a trick of the light if she hadn't been waiting on point.

Sweat tickled her hairline though the temperature outside had dropped hugely since sundown. She shouldn't be hot, but she was . . . even as she was cold. The hairs on her arms stood up with tiny minds of their own while nerves zinged in her skin like live wires.

In the far corner of the compound, she could see flashes of welding light, hear the *whoosh-thwap* of compressed air tools. That noise was enough to mask any the four men were making—four, because Harry had obviously joined the other three.

If the extra man had been Eli, she would've known, a thought that frightened her to admit because of the implications of a connection to him she didn't want or didn't need and refused to try and understand.

Her refusal meant nothing. The connection was there, tugging at her heart in ways that she couldn't have known to anticipate, wasn't sure she could trust, but was suddenly desperate to explore. But this wasn't the time and this wasn't the place, so she concentrated on what was happening instead. Eli had told her to be ready; she would not disappoint.

A loud sound like a jackhammer going off in the shop kept her from hearing much of the noise from the transport as the rear door swung open heavily on its hinges. Seconds later the largest of the men took what looked like a pair of bolt cutters to the lock on the gate and entered the cage.

The sight of these big hulking men materializing out of nowhere in the middle of the night was bound to scare the girls like mad. She wished she could be there with them, could soothe their fears and their worries, yet knew by moving from where she waited she stood a good chance of jeopardizing the rescue's success.

That was the last thing she wanted to do. And so she sat and shivered and sweated, silently praying while she watched Harry make his way deeper into the cage. The girls would know and recognize him; Stella wasn't sure if the familiarity wouldn't spawn more fear than trust, but it wasn't her decision. It wasn't her plan.

He gestured one girl forward from the shelter. The slender teen, dark-haired and barefoot, hesitated, trembling, her trepidation palpable even from where Stella crouched, mumbling, "C'mon, honey. You can trust this one."

At last, Harry won the girl's confidence. Once she reached him, her tiny steps taking forever, he bent down, his face on her level as he spoke. He never touched her, never made any threatening movements. Finally, she nodded and scurried noiselessly back to the shelter.

Seconds later, two girls appeared, running from the shadows, across the ground, and into the transport. Ten seconds crawled by, and Harry, having taken up position at the rear of the trailer, waved two more girls forward. They followed the same path across the square of yard as the others, and Stella began a countdown that seemed endless but in reality was under ten minutes.

All of the girls were out of the cage now and on their way to being returned to their families. Stella didn't even fight the tears as they rolled down her cheeks. She simply held her breath as two of the men secured the trailer and the four of them climbed into the cab, two front and two back.

Three screeching blasts from an air horn and a loud, growling rumble had her turning her head toward the machine shop in time to see Eli backing his way out on foot, directing the driver of a huge diesel rig between the shop's support beams like he would an airplane pilot into a hangar.

The rig had been in the shop for repairs for months, and still it rumbled loud enough to wake the dead, belching plumes of exhaust from dual smokestacks, vibrating the ground it rolled over until she felt the urge to reach out and hold on before both she and her shelter toppled over.

If Eli wanted a distraction, this would have been the distraction to use. With all of Ramon's men working at the back of the compound in the various shops, their attention had been drawn from that direction.

She whipped her gaze back toward the transport rig. She hadn't even heard it start up, yet it had pulled away from the cage and was already halfway through the compound's front gate. Jumping for pure joy was the first thought that came to her mind.

The second was that Eli was still here.

And she was still here.

What was going on?

She got to her feet and walked to the front of the enclosure, grabbing hold of the chain links high overhead.

What the hell was going on?

Now that she stood in the open, she resisted checking the transport's progress and kept her gaze on Eli. She didn't want anyone who saw her to see her looking anywhere else. She was not going to screw up this rescue, not when two dozen plus girls had already been sent out of this compound because of her bad judgment.

The driver cut off the truck's engine then, jumped down from the cab, and engaged Eli in rapid-fire Spanish. Their conversation drifted up on the wind. She made out the single word sabotage as the discussion grew heated. Seconds later, another man joined the fray.

Eli held out both hands and backed away from what appeared to be an impending fight. A third man appeared, gesturing frantically, threateningly, and in the next moment the spotlight on top of the barracks came on to light up the entire back half of the compound yard.

The men stopped, tossed forearms to foreheads, turned their attention from Eli and the truck to the door opening at the barracks' near end. The door to the largest of the rooms. The door through which Ramon Gutierrez had just appeared. Arturo, his lap dog, was immediately at his side, assault rifle at the ready as both men stepped off the porch and headed toward the crowd gathering around Eli.

Instinctively, Stella found herself returning to the dark shadows of the shelter and backing up beneath the overhang. She wanted to see without being seen, to watch the trainwreck unfolding without anyone catching scent of her increasing panic and fear.

Ramon stood facing Eli rather than taking his right-hand man to his side, and Stella tasted the sharp metallic tang of blood where she'd bit the inside of her cheek. Eli would never slip up and get caught . . . unless getting caught *was* the distraction!

Oh God, no!

She crossed her arms tightly over her chest, but it wasn't enough to stop her shaking. He'd had no reason to anticipate her poisoning him, but he'd known *this* was coming. She couldn't believe he was sacrificing himself when he could've found a way to leave with the others.

Unless he was staying for her . . .

Shoulders against the wall, she sank to her haunches and dropped her head back, once, twice, thud, thud, thud, her tears now flowing freely.

He hadn't left because he hadn't had time to free her! The diesel rig hadn't been a distraction as much as a signal for the others to go. He'd been caught or his cover blown or he'd seen no way out. And he'd sent the others on.

The conversation suddenly exploded; she felt the waves of heated accusations from where she sat huddled, and even though Eli's partners were out there and close, fear for his life left her breathless, left her weak and quite certain that in moments her heart would cease to beat.

And at the sound of an approaching helicopter's blades slicing through the air, it did.

Twelve

The sun was peeking over the horizon in hues of orange and red when Stella opened her eyes, in full disbelief that she'd fallen asleep. Considering that her eyes felt like operational gravel pits, she couldn't have dozed more than an hour.

She swung her legs over the plank bench in her shelter, sat up, grabbed her hat from the ground, stood and stretched. She hesitated a moment before stepping from beneath the overhang, taking a moment to pick the fuzz from her subconscious, jerking fully alert when all became clear.

Warren Aceveda had arrived by helicopter at dawn and in time to witness Ramon taking Eli into custody after discovering the missing girls and ditto the transport. She reeled on her boot heels as she'd reeled last night, stepping away from the shelter once she'd found her balance—only to lose it again almost immediately.

Eli stood leaning one shoulder against the chain-link fence inside the cage next to hers. She grabbed hold of her own prison bars and met his gaze. "What happened? I saw Ramon haul you to his office. I sat down to wait and obviously fell asleep."

She could not believe that she'd fallen asleep. "God, Eli. What happened?"

He crossed his arms, tucked his fingers into his pits. "Ramon decided that Rabbit wasn't the only leak in the compound."

He said it in much the same tone one would use to mention they'd scheduled a plumber to visit. "What proof did he have? What evidence?"

"C'mon, Stella. Look at the assholes we're dealing with here," he said, and snorted. "In Ramon's backward world, it's guilty until proven innocent. Present company included. And even then it doesn't matter. He's got a bad side it's best not to cross."

Stella shivered. "And you crossed it."

"Seems so," he said with a shrug.

Why was he such a defeatist? She refused to believe that he'd given up. She wasn't giving up. Not on him. Not on herself. Not on them. "Did you do it on purpose?"

"Do what?"

"Screw up. Get caught."

"Does it matter?"

It mattered to her because of the part she'd played. A part she couldn't keep to herself any longer with all she was feeling. "Of course it matters."

"Why? Why does it matter what I did?" He jerked his chin back over his shoulder, as if reminding her that he was alone in the cage. "The girls are out of here, and the compound's on its way to being history."

"It matters because you shouldn't have had to make the sacrifice," she practically hissed. "You don't deserve to be in here. I do. But not you."

He lifted a brow, but remained silent.

"Eli?"

"Look, Stella." He pushed off the fence, scraped both hands back over his head. "Four guys just drove out of here with two dozen girls. Four guys who've got my back. If bad shit goes down before they return, at least I'll have fixed my royal fuck-up."

She shook her head. No. She wasn't letting him go down thinking he'd done this. Thinking he had anything for which to make amends. "I'm the one who fucked up, Eli. It wasn't you, it was me.

"I wanted to find Carmen and you were in my way. I knew I couldn't get to the compound unless I got rid of you, because every stinking time I turned around, you were there, walking the perimeter, pacing, your big bad self and your big bad gun making it hard to do what I needed to do."

She snorted, her fingers shaking as she pressed them to her throat where her heart thumped like the foot of a deranged bunny. "Talk about a thorn in my side."

He grew still, stiff, a statue steeped in rage. "What are you saying, Stella?"

"I poisoned you." There. It was out. After all this time, it was out, and she felt faint from the mixture of fear and relief. "You left your water at the far corner of the compound. It was easy for me to sneak up the arroyo and"—she gestured weakly—"do what I did."

Eli's cage shook from the force of his sudden angry and deathlike grip. "Stella, goddammit, woman. What the hell were you thinking?"

"Save your story, Miss Banks, for when you and Mr. McKenzie need an interesting topic of conversation in order to keep your minds on this side of sanity."

At the sound of the second male voice, Stella turned to find a man she hadn't seen before walking into the narrow space between the two cages.

He was hard-looking, lean, yet at the same time muscled. He wore clothes similar to Eli's, pocketed fatigues laced into leather combat boots and a dark T-shirt. He also carried a similar gun strapped to his back.

She couldn't see his eyes; he wore sunglasses stylishly at odds with the rest of his soldier-of-fortune costume. And he spoke with an island patois, his long dreadlocks held back from his face with a bandanna.

When he smiled, his white teeth appeared even brighter against his coffee-colored skin. Obviously one of Aceveda's men who'd choppered in with his boss.

"Mr. McKenzie?" she finally thought to ask.

The man laughed. "Eli, *mon*. Did you not tell the lady your true name?"

"I told her what she needed to know," Eli said cruelly.

"How chivalrous of you to protect her." The man glanced from Eli to Stella and back. "Though I can't say much that I blame you on that."

"What do you want?" Eli barked.

"As a rule I am a peace-loving man—"

Eli cut him off with a sharp laugh that had Stella wanting to cower. "You're an assassin."

The man held up one finger. "That is my job title, and I am not defined by my career."

Stella glanced quickly at Eli and found him rolling his eyes. She also found the veins at his temple and those in his neck corded against his skin in sharp relief, and wondered if the two had had a run-in earlier in Ramon's office.

"Yet being a peace-loving man does not mean I don't enjoy the thrill of the hunt."

That said, the man fished into one of his pockets for a thin, square box of dark-papered cigarettes. He lit the one he put to his lips with a match, then pulled from another pocket what appeared to be a pair of wire cutters and began snipping links in the fence keeping her caged.

It was when he moved to Eli's that he said, "The sun is just rising. The heat won't yet be intense, and you can make good time. It will be later when you'll be questioning everything you see, wondering if the horizon is nothing more than a mirage."

He stepped back then, pocketed the tool, and pinched the cigarette from his mouth with an index finger and thumb. He blew a long stream of smoke into the air and frowned at both of them. "Well? What are you waiting for?"

"You're setting us free?" Stella asked.

"Only until I catch you again."

Eli slammed his fist against the cage. "You sick fuck."

"Perhaps," he said, retreating to join the approaching Ramon and the man she assumed was Aceveda. Both had wide smiles on their faces, obviously in on the show. "But I would not be wasting time, if I were in your shoes."

"Who the hell is that man?" Stella asked, falling into step beside Eli.

He didn't want to slow their pace or waste their energy by talking—or by throttling her for what she'd done. And so he answered quickly. "Aceveda's pit bull."

"I don't get it." Her long legs matched his step for step. "Why would he let us go?"

"Exactly the reason he gave. He's going to hunt us down," Eli bit off, wishing for a gun or a knife or even a fucking paper clip. They were on their feet in the desert without a weapon, without shelter, and, worst of all, without water.

"Eli, listen—"

"No." He whirled on her then, steam coming from his nostrils. "I don't have time to listen. If we don't walk in circles, we might make it three miles before he comes after us. But without a compass or GPS device, I can't guarantee that will happen. Which pretty much makes us fucking sitting ducks."

"We have the sun."

"Yeah. The sun." She acted like she'd discovered penicillin. Their only luck with the sun was that it wasn't the middle of August. "And hundreds of square miles of nothing to guide our way."

She reached up and pushed back the brim of her hat. "Well, we might have my truck."

"What?"

She nodded. "How did you think I got here in the first place?"

He didn't want to think about that because her first place

was connected directly to his poisoning, and he was already having a hard time reconciling the woman who'd tried to kill him with the woman he'd fucked like they might have a future.

"Where is it?"

She nodded to indicate the empty landscape behind him. "There's a dry creek bed running out of the arroyo. I drove in on the main road, then cut across the desert parallel to the drive into the compound. A couple of miles, maybe?"

"You can find it from here?"

She glanced in the direction they were headed, glanced in the direction they'd come, glanced at the hard, dry, and dusty surface beneath her feet before looking up to answer. "Yeah, but if we get out of here, we will talk about this."

He stiffened. "About which this? What we did in bed? Where we go from here? Or you wanting me dead?"

All she did was roll her eyes and bump his biceps hard as she pushed passed.

He turned and followed, letting her lead the way but not too happy about it, hoping like hell she knew where she was going and wasn't finishing what she'd started by dropping him off in a scorpion pit.

But the part of him that recognized her as a kindred spirit knew that wasn't the case.

She'd come here with a mission and he'd been in her way—the same way she'd been in his. Because he'd done his job well, she'd had no way of knowing that he wasn't who he seemed. Because she'd done her job well, he'd puked up his guts all the way to Saratoga.

He had to admit a grudging respect for her gutsiness, and one not so grudging for her very fine ass. It was hard not to think about what they'd done in bed with her walking in front of him, her long legs eating up the ground.

He cleared his throat and jogged to catch up. "Having flown in earlier, he might've caught sight of your truck and will start looking there."

"You have another suggestion for getting out of here and fast?" she asked, without looking over.

"No. I'm assuming you didn't drive in here without supplies."

"You assume correctly."

If they were going to survive, they had to work together, not do whatever it was they were doing here, fighting, bickering, comparing the size of their balls. "What do you have? Water?"

She nodded. "Water, yes. And a satellite phone. If it's still in one piece. If the truck's even there."

"I'm betting it is. If they'd found it, they would have hauled it in. And I didn't hear any gloating about it being trashed."

"Not exactly the brightest bulbs on the planet Ramon hired."

He heard the wry humor in her voice, and an easing of the tension. "Let's work on the assumption that your truck is still there. We grab everything that we can and head out on foot ASAP."

This time she did glance over. "On foot. Not in the truck?"

He nodded. "Even if it's running, it's a target."

"And two people on foot are not?"

"Only if they're on foot." He wasn't going to mention thermal imaging at this point. "If your phone is intact, we're good. If not, you said you had a GPS device?"

"I did. I can't say I still do."

"One step at a time. The phone is plan A. The GPS is plan B. We head out, use your tire iron or whatever you have, and dig a couple of shallow graves."

"Graves?"

"I figure that should make you hapwill py."

She swung her arm wide and slammed her fist into his chest. "I never wanted you dead. Just out of the way."

"I know."

She careened to a stop, whirled on him. "You know? That's it? You know?"

"I know why you did it, and I'm still alive." He took off again. "Let's go."

It took her a minute to make up her mind, but then she quickly caught up. "What are you saying?"

"That if I'd been in your place I might have done the same thing. I've certainly done worse." Worse than what most people had it in them to imagine, much less do. "And you'll notice I didn't hesitate to use you."

She walked silently at his side for several minutes, but he could hear the mental gears grinding, hear her boots scuff the hard-packed desert floor, hear the sighs that she made right before asking, "Are you talking about the shower or the sex? Or both?"

This time he was the one who hesitated. The shower was an easy one. He'd needed the distraction and ruthlessly used her. But that ruthlessness had been the catalyst for what had come later. For the wild ride she'd taken him on, as if she'd been using him.

He couldn't answer. He'd let her think what she wanted—that he didn't know, that he didn't want to hurt her. Because he couldn't tell her the truth.

That what they'd done in bed had been the resurrection of his long road back from the dead. And then her truck came into view so he didn't have to tell her a goddamn thing.

Thirteen

Miraculously, the truck was in one piece and exactly where she'd left it. When Ramon's goons had grabbed her, she'd been far enough away that they hadn't spotted it immediately—though why they'd never gone back and searched she couldn't fathom. The bulb and planet thing, she supposed.

Eli had stopped her from starting up the engine to see if they might eventually be able to drive it out of here. They'd come back for it later, he insisted, then gave her a pinky swear when she'd made him promise. This truck had been outfitted to make surveillance a big fat piece of cake, and she did not want to have to start over from scratch.

They were now on foot, an hour away from the compound, carrying her tire iron and her GPS locator. The battery on her phone had, unfortunately, been dead. Eli had tucked it into his fatigues anyway.

His fatigues were now all he wore, as he'd fashioned a pack out of his T-shirt, filled it with her dozen bottles of water, and slung it across his shoulder. He made quite the floor show, half-naked with the butt of her gun riding at the small of his back.

Definitely better scenery than the endless rust-colored

landscape. In fact, she doubted she'd ever tire of looking at him, or talking with him, or opening up beneath him and taking him into her body.

She'd been lying when she'd told him she'd rather be touched by no one, because she wanted to be touched and wanted by him. She wanted to learn all there was to learn, know all there was to know. He made her laugh, and he made her cry, and he made her heart pitter-patter all over the place. And that was enough for now.

She'd gone a half dozen steps, thinking about how to convince him to stick around and see how they fit in real life, before realizing he'd stopped. Turning back, she found him studying the creek bed they'd followed.

Where they stood, there was a definite incline of sorts on one side, and he said, "We'll stop here."

And why not? The dirt was already crumbling. He could more easily dig out a place for them to hide and hopefully avoid being seen should the chopper fly over. "The better to bury me with, my dear?"

"Your choice," he said, the strange words bringing up her gaze. "One grave or two?"

It felt like a test, his question, the look in his eyes that seemed strangely tender. God, she must be delirious from heat stroke, except she wasn't overly hot.

"Whatever's quicker, easier, and safer," she said, because she knew it was too soon to say more.

"My kinda woman. Damn the flirtation, full steam ahead." He stuffed the GPS into a pocket, unloaded his water pack, and set to work digging, leaving her struggling with what he'd just said.

Struggling, until she couldn't do so alone any longer. "Eli?"

His head was down, muffling his responding, "Stella?"

"If you were flirting with me, I lost it."

"That's okay," he said way too quickly.

"No, it's not okay." She squatted beside him, worried her hat in her hands. "Guys don't flirt with me. Either I turn them off or I put them off. Even guys I haven't poisoned. And I'm not sure why."

He snorted, the sound strangely soft. "Trust me. I don't know a man alive who'd be turned off by anything about you."

"I can be bossy. And mouthy. And I pretty much hate being told what to do."

"Nothing wrong with any of that."

"There is if you're a guy who likes a woman to do what you say without asking questions."

"Well, I'm not." Gruff this time, not soft at all. "So give it a rest."

And there he went telling her what to do. "I don't put you off, then?"

"Only when you keeping talking while I'm trying to save our lives."

"If you'd let me help, I'd be too busy to be nervous and I'd be easier to shut up."

He sat back on his knees then, and stared at her for what seemed like forever. Beads of sweat pooled at the base of his throat, and she couldn't help it. She reached out and swiped them away with her fingers.

He grabbed her wrist before she drew back. "I'm not trying to shut you up, Stella. If it helps to talk, then talk. It doesn't put me off. And it's sure as hell not going to turn me off. But that's one thing this isn't the time or place to discuss."

He let her go then, as if satisfied that what he'd said had sunk in. She wasn't sure that it had. She was still feeling his fingers where they'd branded her skin.

He was back to digging and she was back to watching the amazing flex of his muscles at work when she thought to ask, "Later, then? When we're away from here? We can talk about it then? Another pinky swear?"

"Anything you want, sweetheart. We can talk about anything you want."

He'd called her sweetheart. She wondered if he realized it, or if he was only humoring her, or if he might possibly like her enough to want to learn to like her more. To one day love her the way she was wondering about loving him.

She opened her mouth, wanting to say something, to ask, to even have him assure her that he wasn't feeding her a lot of bullshit to keep her sane. But she was stopped from saying anything by the approaching *thwap-thwap-thwap* of a helicopter's blades.

Oh God. Oh God. Oh God, no!

Trembling, she pushed up to her feet. At her side, Eli did the same, swearing under his breath as he slammed the tire iron to the ground. Stella couldn't help it. She backed up into him, her shoulder tucked to his armpit, and grasped his hand where it hung at her hip.

He squeezed hard, his palm sweaty, his fingers threading with hers, shaking slightly. He braced his forearm across her chest as the chopper drew near. She could feel the thunder of his heart in rhythmic pulses along her back.

And when he dropped his chin to her shoulder and rubbed his cheek to hers, she knew there was no one else who could've made her feel so safe with the Grim Reaper dropping into her lap. As the chopper descended, she reached up with her free hand to hold her hat in place. She couldn't speak, barely managed to pray, and only that because of how tightly Eli held her.

When the door to the chopper opened and Aceveda's man stepped out, jogging out from beneath the rotors and gesturing them forward, Stella wasn't sure whether to move or to vomit or simply wait for him to pull out a gun and mow them both to the ground.

Wait! A gun! Eli had her gun!

She unlaced their fingers, reached around behind him,

and patted the small of his back above the pistol's grip. He shook his head slowly, the gesture more to let her know not to move swiftly than one telling her to back away.

"I'm going to see what he wants," he said under his breath but still loud enough for her to hear.

"What?" Oh, no. She couldn't deal with him leaving her here.

"Stella, listen," he said, turning his head, not his body, to face her. "If he'd planned to shoot us on sight, he would have. If he wanted to herd us into the chopper, he'd be waving a gun, not his arm."

"He works for Aceveda, Eli. He can't want anything good."

He reached up, tucked back loose strands of hair behind her ear. "I know, sweetheart. But I've got a niggling suspicion we're not seeing the whole picture here."

"I swear," she said, grabbing his belt loops and shaking him. "If you get yourself killed and leave me here with him, I'll never speak to you again."

Laughing, he dropped a kiss on the end of her nose. "And I'll be man enough to forgive you anyway," he said with a wink before sobering. "I'm going to step in front of you, and I want you to take the gun."

"No, Eli—"

"We're doing this my way, Stella." His scowl was fierce, yet tender. "If you have the gun, I'll know you're safe and I can focus on what I have to do. Okay?"

She hated to, but she nodded.

"All right. I'm going." He held up both hands, showing the pilot he was approaching unarmed. As he crossed into her path, she lifted the Walther P99 from his waistband, tucked it into her own.

The pilot started towards him, and the two men met halfway between where she stood and the chopper. She watched as they talked, and talked comfortably, any tension from earlier seemingly absent. Whatever the hell was going on, she didn't like it at all. And she especially didn't like it when the two men shook hands.

Eli glanced back toward her and gestured. The pilot nodded and grinned. The man actually grinned, and that was when she began to pace, wondering what the two had to discuss in such detail, and if Eli was this chatty with all assassins. Or just this one and her.

When he motioned her forward, she hesitated, dozens of scenarios running through her mind on fast-forward. It was the weight of the gun in the small of her back that finally gave her strength. Managing to put one foot in front of the other, she ran, ducking beneath the whirring blades.

Eli grabbed her and pulled her close briefly. She breathed him in and, feeling better, allowed the two men to help her up and into the tiny jump seat behind the pilot's, trusting that Eli knew what he was doing.

He exchanged even more words with the other man before following her in, buckling himself into the front passenger seat. The pilot boarded, gave Eli another wide smile, a cheery thumbs-up, and lifted off.

Stella closed her eyes and took a deep breath, looking up only after they were in flight. The props were so loud she couldn't think to hear, or hear to think, or do anything but watch the desert floor zoom by as they followed the creek bed the rest of the way to the main road.

And then followed the main road away from the compound.

What the hell was going on?

Without looking, Eli reached back to take her hand. She gripped his with both of hers, sensing less tension in his body than she had before. They flew on longer than she'd expected, and finally began to descend in what appeared to be the middle of nowhere. Eli gave her leg one last pat then focused on the ground below.

Aceveda's pilot set the chopper down without incident and shut off the engine. Within seconds, Stella's ears began to ring from the silence and the echo of her fast-beating heart. Had he brought them here to kill them, or what? Both men opened their doors, and Eli reached back to help her out.

She followed him to the front of the helicopter and across the road from where they'd set down. She held tight to his hand, frowning when he bent close and whispered, "I'll tell you everything in a minute, but Ezra's got something he wants us to see."

All she could do was trust him and wonder even more about the man named Ezra. Standing as she was between the two men, she followed the direction he pointed. Clueless, she watched the mirage-like waves shimmer on the horizon and then—

Boom!

A huge orange fireball mushroomed upward. Flames licked the sky between tongues of rising black smoke. Smaller explosions followed until the fire and thick burn-off could have easily been used as a beacon.

And then the repercussion of what she was seeing struck. "The compound!"

"Such a beautiful site, she is," Ezra said. "All that power and fury. And so much evil wiped out with no more than a properly timed fuse."

"You're responsible for that?" she gasped, backing a step closer to Eli.

"That I am, Miss Stella. That I am."

"But . . . why?" Wasn't he the bad guy?

"What is wrong?" he asked, frowning. "I thought you would be pleased to see such evil brought to an end."

She couldn't believe it. He almost looked crushed. "Of course I'm pleased. I'm just surprised. And more than a little bit leery."

He held up one finger and his smile returned. "Ah, but remember what I said earlier today. I am a man not defined by my career."

Eli reached out and offered his hand. "Thanks, Ezra. We owe you."

"No, my friend." He enclosed Eli's hand in both of his own. "You owe me naught."

Stella looked from one to the other. "That's it? You're leaving us here?"

"You'll be fine here, Miss Stella. Trust me on this. And trust your Mr. McKenzie." Bowing slightly, Ezra turned and jogged back across the road, his dreadlocks flying like ropes behind him.

Once he'd put the chopper into the air, lifting off with a wave, she collapsed into Eli's arms, her hat falling to the ground, snuggling up to his bare chest with a shudder. "Who in the hell is that man?"

Eli's arms came tightly around her. "Beyond the fact that he's wearing a ring from the United States Naval Academy, I'm not exactly sure."

"I can't believe it. It's over. This entire bad dream is over."

He nuzzled his face to the top of her head. "All except this part."

"This part?"

He nodded, dropping kisses along her hairline. "Being stuck in the middle of nowhere."

"But he said we'd be all right here."

"And you trust him?"

Alarm shot through her. "He let us go."

"Yeah. There is that," Eli said. "And then there is this."

"This?" she asked, but then she didn't need him to answer. She heard it. The same truck that had left the compound earlier pulling the transport trailer was now unencumbered and headed straight their way. Eli's friends had obviously delivered the girls to safety.

She couldn't believe the relief rushing through her limbs, tingling and tickling, making her want to laugh and to weep and to pee. Doing what she'd sworn to never do, she leaned onto a man for strength, sagging back against Eli.

He wrapped his arms around her middle, and they watched the truck come to a stop. The four men climbed out and walked toward them. Stella straightened, and Eli hooked his elbow around her neck. "Stella, you know Harry van Zandt."

"Hey, Stella," Harry said, and she lifted a hand shyly in an answering wave.

Eli then pointed to the others. "This is Julian Samms"— the one with the longest hair offered a silent nod—"Kelly John Beach"—the largest of the three men grinned—"and Mick Savin"—the one with the wicked tattoo on the back of his neck gave her a quick salute—"my brothers-in-arms."

"It's nice to meet all of you," she said, listening to the rumble of male voices as they all began to talk. To her. To one another. To Eli. She didn't say a word after that, just basked in the warm air and testosterone and the biggest safety net she'd ever known.

It was when the men turned for the truck that she held Eli back.

He looked down at her. "What's up?"

"You made a pinky swear."

"I did?" he asked, brows arched in innocence.

"You did. That we can talk. That you won't drop me off in Del Rio and disappear from my life," she said, punching him lightly in the ribs.

"Oh, that." He rested his forehead on hers, his forearms on her shoulders, and laced his hands. "You have a problem with skipping Del Rio altogether?"

"What do you mean?" she asked, feeling the bulge of her heart in her throat.

"I've got to check in with the head honcho in New York."

"New York?"

He nodded. "I thought you might like to go shopping. Nothing personal, but I'm really sick of seeing you in these clothes."

"*You're* sick of them. Try wearing them as long as I've been." She was smiling so broadly her face hurt. "I think they're ready to walk across the border on their own."

"Then it's a deal? You'll come to New York and we'll see what happens?"

"Are you kidding? Say the word and I'm there."

"How's this for a word?" he asked, and he kissed her. Kissed her in the middle of the road with his buddies whooping and jeering and honking the horn.

Kissed her like he'd never get enough, like no other woman had existed before, like she was all he would ever want in his life.

She liked that, and so she kissed him back just the same, finally pulling away to sigh and whisper, "I like that word a lot. And you say it so well."

"You ain't seen nothin' yet, baby."

Epilogue

Red sand covering his Hugo Boss loafers and the cuffs of his matching black linen pants, Warren Aceveda raised a hand to shield his eyes, already shaded by a sleek pair of Emporio Armani's.

He searched the smoke-filled horizon, relaxing in the shade of the Jeep Ramon Gutierrez had instructed his driver to use to chase down the transport.

The driver lay slumped over the wheel, a single gunshot wound piercing the base of his skull. Ramon slumped similarly, halfway out the door, held in place by the seatbelt he'd insisted on wearing. He'd taken his bullet to the temple.

Warren disliked killing men before they had fulfilled their purpose. Ramon would have had many more years to devote to Spectra IT had he not bungled things here so badly.

He was no more a leader than had been Peter Deacon, Warren's predecessor.

Both men had been ruthlessly deceived by the so-called elite members of the Smithson Group. Warren's superiors were rapidly losing patience with the rogue mercenaries employed by Hank Smithson.

As it was, Warren himself would be seeing to the group's

destruction soon enough. For now, however, he had business to attend to in New Mexico.

And to help him carry it out, he mused with moderate amusement, watching as Ezra and the chopper came into view, his own private branch of the armed forces.

*Meet the men of the Smithson Group—five spies whose best work is done in the field and between the sheets. Smart, built, trained to do everything well—and that's everything—they're the guys you want on your side of the bed. Go deep undercover? No problem. Take out the bad guys? Done. Play by the rules? I don't think so. Indulge a woman's every fantasy? Happy to please, ma'am.
Fall in love? Hey, even a secret agent's got his weak spots . . .*

Bad boys. Good spies. Unforgettable lovers.

Episode One:
THE BANE AFFAIR
by
Alison Kent

"Smart, funny, exciting, touching, and *hot*."
—Cherry Adair

"Fast, dangerous, sexy."—Shannon McKenna

<u>Get started with Christian Bane, SG–5</u>

Christian Bane is a man of few words, so when he talks, people listen. One of the Smithson Group's elite force, Christian's also the walking wounded, haunted by his past. Something about being betrayed by a woman, then left to die in a Thai prison by the notorious crime syndicate Spectra IT gives a guy demons. But now, Spectra has made a secret deal with a top scientist to crack a governmental encryption technology, and Christian has his orders: Pose as Spectra boss Peter Deacon. Going deep undercover as the slick womanizer will be tough for Christian. Getting cozy with the scientist's beautiful goddaughter, Natasha, to get information won't be. But the closer he gets to Natasha, the harder it gets to deceive her. She's so alluring, so trusting, so completely unexpected he suspects someone's been giving out faulty intel. If Natasha isn't the criminal he was led to believe, they're both being played for fools. Now, with Spectra closing in, Christian's best chance for survival is to confront his demons and trust the only one he can . . . Natasha.

Available from Brava in October 2004.

**Episode Two:
THE SHAUGHNESSEY ACCORD
by
Alison Kent**

Get hot and bothered with Tripp Shaughnessey, SG–5

When someone screams Tripp Shaughnessey's name, it's usually a woman in the throes of passion or one who's just caught him with his hand in the proverbial cookie jar. Sometimes it's both. Tripp is sarcastic, fun-loving, and funny, with a habit of seducing every woman he says hello to. But the one who really gets him hot and bothered is Glory Brighton, the curvaceous owner of his favorite sandwich shop. The nonstop banter between Glory and Tripp has been leading up to a full-body kiss in the back storeroom. And that's just where they are when all hell breaks loose. Glory's past includes some very bad men connected to Spectra, men convinced she may have important intel hidden in her place. Now, with the shop under siege, and gunmen holding customers hostage, Tripp shows Glory his true colors: He's no sweet, rumpled "engineer" from the Smithson Group, but a well-trained, hard-core covert op whose easygoing rep is about to be put to the test . . .

Available from Brava in November 2004.

Episode Three:
THE SAMMS AGENDA
by
Alison Kent

Get down and dirty with Julian Samms, SG–5

From his piercing blue eyes to his commanding presence, everything about Julian Samms says all-business and no bull. He expects a lot from his team—some say too much. But that's how you keep people alive, by running things smooth, clean, and quick. Under Julian's watch, that's how it plays. Except today. The mission was straightforward: Extract Katrina Flurry, ex-girlfriend of deposed Spectra boss Peter Deacon, from her Miami condo before a hit man can silence her for good. But things didn't go according to plan, and Julian's suddenly on the run with a woman who gives new meaning to high maintenance. Stuck in a cheap motel with a force of nature who seems determined to get them killed, Julian can't believe his luck. Katrina is infuriating, unpredictable, adorable, and possibly the most exciting, sexy woman he's ever met. A woman who makes Julian want to forget his playbook and go wild, spending hours in bed. And on the off-chance that they don't get out alive, Julian's new live-for-today motto is starting right now . . .

Available from Brava in December 2004.

Episode Four:
THE BEACH ALIBI
by
Alison Kent

Get deep undercover with Kelly John Beach, SG–5

Kelly John Beach is the go-to guy known for covering all the bases and moving in the shadows like a ghost. But now, the ultimate spy is in big trouble: during his last mission, he was caught breaking into a Spectra IT high-rise on one of their video surveillance cameras. The SG–5 team has to make an alternate tape fast, one that proves K.J. was elsewhere at the time of the break-in. The plan is simple: Someone from Smithson will pose as K.J.'s lover, and SG–5's strategically placed cameras will record their every intimate, erotic encounter in elevators, theater hallways, and other daring forums. But Kelly John never expects that "alibi" to come in the form of Emma Webster, the sexy coworker who has starred in so many of his not-for-prime-time fantasies. Getting his hands—and anything else he can—on Emma under the guise of work is a dream come true. Deceiving the good-hearted, trusting woman isn't. And when Spectra realizes that the way to K.J. is through Emma, the spy is ready to come in from the cold, and show her how far he'll go to protect the woman he loves . . .

Available from Brava in January 2005.

Episode Five:
THE McKENZIE ARTIFACT
by
Alison Kent

Get what you came for with Eli McKenzie, SG–5

Five months ago, SG–5 operative Eli McKenzie was in deep cover in Mexico, infiltrating a Spectra ring that kidnaps young girls and sells them into a life beyond imagining. Not being able to move on the Spectra scum right away was torture for the tough-but-compassionate superspy. But that wasn't the only problem—someone on the inside was slowly poisoning Eli, clouding his judgment and forcing him to make an abrupt trip back to the Smithson Group's headquarters to heal. Now, Eli's ready to return . . . with a vengeance. It seems his quick departure left a private investigator named Stella Banks in some hot water. Spectra operatives have nabbed the nosy Stella and are awaiting word on how to handle her disposal. Eli knows the only way to save her life and his is to reveal himself to Stella and get her to trust him. Seeing the way Stella takes care of the frightened girls melts Eli's armor, and soon, they find that the best way to survive this brutal assignment is to steal time in each other's arms. It's a bliss Eli's intent on keeping, no matter what he has to do to protect it. Because Eli McKenzie has unfinished business with Spectra—and with the woman who has renewed his heart—this is one man who always finishes what he starts . . .

Available from Brava in February 2005.

Please sample other books
in this wonderful series:
Available right now—
THE BANE AFFAIR

Christian watched the road rush by beneath the car, the roar in his ears much more than that of the engine or the tires. He should have trusted his instincts earlier. Susan's turning green wasn't about the amount of alcohol left in her system at all.

He held out his right hand, gripped the steering wheel with his left. "Hand me your phone."

"Why?"

"The phone, Natasha." He didn't have time to argue. Didn't have time to explain. Had time to do nothing but react. An exit loomed to the right. He downshifted to slow the car and swerved across two lanes to take it. Ahead and behind, the road was blessedly free of traffic. "The phone, now, please."

"I don't think so," she said, yelping when he reached across and grabbed it out of her hand.

She slumped defiantly into her seat, arms crossed over her chest. Checking again for oncoming vehicles, he pried open the phone and removed the battery, tossed the case over the top of the car toward the ditch, the power supply to the side of the road a quarter mile away.

"What the hell are you doing?" she screamed, whirling

on him, fists flying, nails raking, grabbing for the steering wheel.

He hit the brakes, whipped into the skid. The fast stop and shoulder strap slammed her back into the bucket. He kept her there with the barrel of the Ruger .45-caliber he snatched from beneath his seat. "Sit down. Nothing's going to happen to you if you sit down and be still."

She didn't say a word, but he heard her hyperventilating panic above the roar in his ears.

"Calm down, Natasha. Listen to me. No one's going to get hurt." His pulse pounded. His mind whirred. "I just need you to be still and be quiet."

"You're pointing a gun at me and you want me to be still and be quiet? You fucking piece of shit." She swiped back the hair from her face. "Don't tell me to be still and be quiet. In fact, don't tell me anything at all. When Susan doesn't hear from me later, she's calling the cops. She knows exactly where we are and what we're driving. So whatever the hell you think you're doing here, you're not getting away with it. You lying, fucking bastard."

He caught her gaze, saw the glassy fear, the damp tears she wouldn't shed, the delineated vessels in the whites of her eyes like a road map penned in red. He wanted to tell her the truth, that he was one of the good guys, to reassure her that she could trust him, that no harm would come her way—but he couldn't tell her any of that and he refused to compound his sins with yet another lie.

And so he issued a growling order. "Shut the hell up, Natasha. Now."

Grabbing his phone from his belt, he punched in a preset code. The phone rang once. Julian Samms picked up the other end. "Shoot."

"I need to get to the farm. Where's Briggs?"

"Hang," Julian ordered, and Christian waited while his SG-5 partner contacted Hank's chopper pilot, waited and watched Natasha hug herself with shaking hands, tears finally and silently rolling down her cheeks.

"I've got you on GPS. Briggs can be there in thirty, but you need to bank the car. And he needs a place to land. Hang."

More waiting. More looking for approaching cars. More watching Natasha glare, shake, and cry.

Christian switched from handset to earphone and lowered the gun to his thigh, keeping his gaze on Natasha while waiting for Julian's instructions. She seemed so small, so wounded, and he kicked himself all over again for failing to make it clear that their involvement was purely physical.

He should have spelled that out from day one, made it more clear that Peter Deacon took trophies, not lovers. But he'd never given her any such warning. Not that it would've done any good. Hell, he knew the lay of the land and here he was, so tied up in knots over what he was putting her through that he couldn't even think straight.

"My name is Christian Bane," he finally said, owing her that much. "That's all I can tell you right now."

She snorted, flipped him the bird, and turned to stare out her window.

"Bane."

"Yeah." Hand to his earpiece, he turned his attention back to Julian.

"Two miles ahead on the right," Julian said as Christian shifted into gear and accelerated, "there's a cutoff. Through a gate. Looks like a dirt road, rutted as hell."

He brought the car up to speed, scanned the landscape. "Got it," he said, and made the turn, nearly bottoming out on the first bump.

"Half a mile, make another right. Other side of a stand of trees."

"Almost there." He reached the cutoff and turned again, caught sight of the tumbledown barn and stables, the flat pasture beyond. Perfect. Plenty of room for the chopper and cover for the car. "Tell Briggs we're waiting."

A short couple of seconds, and Julian said, "He says make it twenty. K.J.'s with him. He'll bring back the car. I'll keep the line open. Hank's expecting you."

"Thanks, J."

Christian maneuvered the Ferrari down the road that wasn't much more than a trail of flattened grass leading to a clearing surrounding the barn. Once he'd circled behind it, he tugged the wire from his ear, cut the engine, and pocketed the keys. When he opened his door, Natasha finally looked over.

"Going someplace?" she asked snidely.

"We both are," he bit back. "Get out."

"You can go to hell, but I'm not going anywhere."

"Actually, you are. And you're going with me." He reminded her that he was the one with the gun.

She got out of the car, slammed the door, and was off like a rocket back down the road. Shit, shit, shit. He checked the safety, shoved the Ruger into his waistband next to the SIG, and took off after her. She was fast, but he was faster. He closed in, but she never slowed, leaving him no choice.

He grabbed her arm. She spun toward him. He took her to the ground, bracing himself for the blow. He landed hard on his shoulder, doing what he could to cushion her fall. She grunted at the impact, and he rolled on top of her, pinning her to the ground with his weight and his strength.

Her adrenaline made for a formidable foe. She shoved at his chest, pummeled him with her fists when he refused to move. He finally had no choice but to grab her wrists, stretch out her arms above her head, hold her there.

Rocks and dirt and twigs bit into his fingers. He knew she felt the bite in the backs of her hands, but still he straddled her, capturing her legs between his.

"You want to wait like this? Twenty minutes? Because we can." His chest heaved in sync with the rapid rise and fall of hers. "Or we can get up and wait at the car. I'm good either way. You tell me."

"Get off me." She spat out the words.

He rolled up and away, kept his hands on her wrists and pulled her to her feet. Then he tugged her close, making sure he had her full attention, ignoring the stabbing pain in his shoulder that didn't hurt half as much as the one in his gut. "I'm not going to put up with any shit here, Natasha. Both of our lives are very likely in danger."

"Oh, right. I can see that. You being the one with the gun and all." She jerked her hands from his.

He let her go, walking a few feet behind her as she made her way slowly back to the barn and the parked car. She had nowhere to run; hopefully, he'd made his point. He had no intention to harm her, no *reason* to harm her, but he needed to finish this job, to make sure Spectra didn't get their hands on whatever it was Bow had to sell.

And now that he'd been stupid enough to get his cover blown . . .

"Where are you taking me?" She splayed shaking palms over the Ferrari's engine bay, staring down at her skin, which was ghostly pale against the car's black sheen.

"To get the answers you've been asking for," he said, guilt eating him from the inside out, and looked up with no small bit of relief at the *thwup-thwup-thwup* of an approaching chopper.

And also available from Brava—

THE SHAUGHNESSEY ACCORD

Tripp grabbed Glory by the shoulders, twirled her bodily across the room and into a tight corner where two of the shelving units met at a right angle.

"I know this part," she whispered as he wedged her inside. "Stay put."

He nodded, drew his gun and pressed his back to the wall at her side. The door slammed open and bounced off the cinderblocks behind. Tripp held the weapon raised, both hands at the ready, his heart doing a freight train run in his chest.

Beside him, Glory barely breathed. The shelf of supplies to his right blocked his view of the door but didn't keep his nostrils from flaring, his neck hairs from bristling, his adrenaline from pumping like gasoline.

He sensed their visitor long before the black-garbed man swung around and aimed his gun straight at Glory's head. The intruder stepped over his own downed associate and held out a gloved hand.

"Give me the gun and she will not die."

Tripp cursed violently under his breath, weighing his options on a different scale than he would've used in this situation had Glory not been involved.

If he'd had time to do more than react, time to think,

plot and plan, he would've stashed the gun behind a can of olives and used the butt end to up his own prisoner count when the time was right.

Instead, he found himself surrendering the very piece that would've gone a long way to protecting Glory from this thug. But he was stuck using nothing but the wits that never seemed to operate at full throttle unless he had a contingency plan.

Right now all he had was a gut full of bile. That and a big fat regret that he didn't think better on his feet than he did.

Having passed over the gun, he raised both hands, palms out. "Let's neither of us go off half-cocked here."

The other man considered him for a long, strange moment, his black eyes broadcasting zero emotion while he stared for what seemed like forever before he tugged the ski mask from his head.

He was young. Tripp would've guessed twenty-three, twenty-four. Except when he looked at the kid's eyes. His expression was so dark, so blank, so unfeeling that it was like looking at a long-dead corpse.

Without moving his gaze from Tripp's, the kid shouted sharp orders in Vietnamese. Two other similarly garbed goons entered the storeroom and dragged away the dead weight Tripp had left in the middle of the floor.

Once the cast of extras was gone, the lead player planted his feet and shifted his gaze between Tripp and Glory, both hands hanging at his sides, one worrying the ski mask into a black fabric ball, the other flexed and ready and holding the gun.

"An interesting situation we find ourselves in here, isn't it?" he finally asked. "Miss Brighton, would you introduce me to your friend?"

"What do you want?" she asked before Tripp could stop her. "Tell me what you want. I'll give it to you, and you can get out of my shop."

His black hair fell over his brow. "If what I have come for was so easily obtained, then I would have it in my possession by now."

He was after whatever the courier from the diamond exchange had delivered to the Spectra agent. Tripp was sure of it. Was sure as well the information would detail future packets removed from Sierra Leone.

The ski mask fell to the floor. "I'm waiting, Miss Brighton."

"He's a friend. A customer." Her hands fluttered at her waist. "We're just . . . good friends."

"You allow all your customers to visit your storeroom?" His mouth twisted cruelly. "Or only the ones with whom you are intimate?"

Glory gasped. Tripp placed his arm in front of her, a protective barrier he knew did little good. "C'mon, man. There's no need to go there."

The Asian kid raised a brow. "Actually, I think there is. Getting what I want often requires me to explore a defense's most vulnerable link. It is not always pleasant, but it can be quite effective."

Tripp was pissed and rapidly getting more so. "Well, there are no links here to explore. So do as the lady suggested. Take what you've come for and let us all get back to our lives."

"Were it only so simple," he said as he gestured Glory forward. She forced her way past the barricade of Tripp's arm. "But we seem to have hit what will no doubt be an endlessly long impasse thanks to one of Miss Brighton's customers."

Glory looked from the kid back to Tripp, her eyes asking questions to which he had zero answers. "I don't understand."

"You are very predictable, Miss Brighton. As is your customer base. Same sandwiches. Same lunch hours. That made planning this job quite easy. I'm assuming the courier using your place of business for a drop point found your tight schedule advantageous, too."

Tripp's mind raced like the wind. The kid was talking way too much. His gang had blacked out the shop's single security camera, had made entry without alerting anyone to their presence, had secured the scene and done it all while Tripp made love to Glory.

Trip had been monitoring the shop for weeks and he'd never noticed the shop being scouted. He hadn't been wise to the intrusion until the kid had shot the lock off the door.

A guy who followed through on such flawless planning didn't start yapping his flap unless he felt there would be no survivors but him. And Tripp had a feeling they were looking into the dead eyes of an animal who'd fight to the death before being taken alive.

Here's a preview of

THE SAMMS AGENDA

South Miami, Friday, 3:30 P.M.

Julian hit the ground with a jolt, seams ripping, bones crunching, joints popping as he rolled to his feet and came up into a full-throttle run.

Coattails flying, he sprinted across the pool's cement deck, hurdled the shattered planter, and gave Katrina no chance to do more than gasp as he grabbed her upper arm and ran.

"Go! Go! Go! Go! Go!"

He propelled her forward, knowing he could run a hell of a lot faster then she could, the both of them dragged down even more by the *slap, slap, slap* of her ridiculous shoes.

She seemed to reach the very same conclusion at the very same time, however, and kicked off the slides to run in bare feet.

Once across the deck and up the courtyard stairs, he shoved open the enclosure's gate. Another bullet ricocheted off the iron railing.

Katrina screamed, but kept up with the pace he set as they pushed through and barreled down the arched walkway toward the parking garage.

Her Lexus was closer, but he doubted she had her keys

and didn't have time to stop, ask, and wait for her to dig them from the bottom of her bag.

Even breaking in, hot-wiring would take longer than the additional burst of speed and extra twenty-five yards they'd need to reach his Benz.

"My car. Let's go," he ordered.

She followed, yelping once, cursing once, twice, yet sticking by his side all the way.

A shot cracked the pavement to the right of their path, a clean shot straight between two of the garage's support beams. Way too close for comfort.

Rivers's practice was about to make perfect in ways Julian didn't want to consider.

The keyless transponder in his pocket activated the entry into his car from three feet away. He touched the handle, jerked open the SL500's driver's side door.

Katrina scrambled across the console, tossed her bag onto the floor; he slid down into his seat, punched the ignition button, shoved the transmission into reverse.

Tires screaming, he whipped backwards out of the parking space and shot down the long row of cars. He hit the street ass-backwards, braked, spun, shifted into first, and floored it, high-octane adrenaline fueling his flight.

Halfway down Grand, several near misses and an equal number of traffic violations later, he cast a quick sideways glance at Katrina and nodded. "You might want to buckle up."

She cackled like she'd never heard anything more ridiculous. "You're suggesting that now?"

He shrugged, keeping an eye on his rearview and any unwanted company, whether Rivers or the cops. He wasn't about to stop for either. "Better late than never."

That earned him a snort, but she did as she'd been told. Then she lifted her left foot into her lap, giving him an eyeful of a whole lotta tanned and toned thigh. "I've got glass in my foot."

He didn't say anything. He had to get out of her neighborhood and ditch his car—a reality that seriously grated. "Stitches?"

She shook her head, leaning down for a closer look at the damage. "I don't think so. Tweezers, antibiotic ointment, and a bandage should suffice."

"I've got a first aid kit in the trunk." How many times had he patched himself up on the fly? "I'll grab it as soon as we stop. In the meantime . . ." He pulled his handkerchief from his pocket.

"Thanks." She halved it into a triangle and wrapped her foot securely, knotting the fabric on top at the base of her toes. "When you hit 95, head south. The police station's on Sunset."

He nodded, turned north at the next intersection.

"Uh, hello? I said Sunset. South, not north."

"I heard you." This wasn't the time for a long explanation as to why he couldn't go to the police, why SG-5 couldn't risk exposure, why he'd learned a long time ago that actions spoke a hell of a lot louder than words.

"Look," she said, settling her sunglasses that he happened to know were Kate Spade firmly in place. "I appreciate the save, even if I was dumb as a stick to get in this car not knowing who you are. But we're going to the police, or I'll be making a scene like you wouldn't believe."

Oh, he believed Miss High Maintenance capable of just that. So far the only surprise had been her lack of complaints over their full out hundred-yard dash and the injury she'd sustained in the process.

"This isn't a police matter." Still, heading in the direction of the station might keep Rivers at bay and give Julian time to consider his options.

"And why would that be?" she asked, her incredulous tone of voice unable to mask the sound of the gears whirring in her mind. "You're with the shooter, aren't you? This kidnapping was the goal all along. You sonofabitch."

Julian couldn't help it. He smiled. It was something he

rarely did for good reason, and the twitch of unused facial muscles felt strange.

But there was just something about a woman with a sailor's mouth that grabbed hold of his gut and twisted him up with the possibilities.

He hadn't had a really good mouth in a very long time.

A thought that sobered him right up. "No. I'm not with the shooter. His name is Benny Rivers. He's with Spectra IT and he's in Miami to take you out."

And here's a peek at

THE BEACH ALIBI

He couldn't believe it.

He abso-fucking-lutely couldn't believe this was happening. Not here. Not now. No way.

He'd prepped for this mission for weeks. He knew every way into this building, every way out. Windows, elevators, ducts, doors, all of it.

He'd wallpapered his workstation with blueprints and surveillance photos, for fuck's sake.

How the hell could he have missed the goddamn camera hidden in the goddamn wall clock?

Kelly John Beach averted his head, stared at his black, rubber-soled shoes, at the pine green and navy leaf pattern in the executive suite's carpet beneath, and ordered himself to think, think.

Think!

The camera was new. The clock hadn't been here earlier tonight. He'd scanned this office an hour after the cleaning crew had left, doing an electronic sweep while in uniform as building security.

There had been nothing—*nothing*—on that wall other than the portrait of the company's founder. That didn't change the fact that now, at 2200, there was. Or the fact that the position he was in was more than compromising.

It was neck-in-the-noose illegal.

Proving that Marian Diamonds was working with the international crime syndicate Spectra IT to smuggle conflict diamonds out of Sierra Leone would hardly negate a breaking-and-entering or burglary charge.

Especially since explaining how he'd come to be in possession of such intel would put the Smithson Group at risk for exposure—exposure he couldn't let happen. That he *wouldn't* let happen . . . think, think.

Think!

The USB flash drive detailing the diamond shipments and subsequent buyers was now tucked safely into a pocket of the vest strapped to his chest, along with the rest of the tools of his highly suspect trade.

Getting out of here wasn't going to be a problem. He'd simply reverse the trip he'd made coming in. No, the trouble would come later.

Three minutes from now, he'd be ground level wearing street clothes. Give the cops another thirty, he'd be wearing handcuffs.

God-fucking-damn.

Sweat beaded on his forehead, rolled like Niagara down his spine. His eyeballs burned. His temples throbbed. His heart was a fist-sized red rubber ball clogging the base of his throat.

Plain and simple, he had to get to the SG-5 ops center without hitting the street. The only way to do that was the train at the Broad Street station. Then underground.

He hated going underground. He hated the dark. Hated the rats. Hated the stench of shit and decay and all the rotten crap he'd have to step in.

Fuck me blind. He growled, grumbled, snorted. Now he was really looking forward to the trip. But a man had to do what a man had to do, or so went the saying.

And so he did. Sucked it up, swallowed his own bullshit along with the red rubber ball, and walked out of the office like the fucking president of the U. S. of A.

"Slow it down, son. Slow it down." Hank Smithson gestured toward Kelly John with the stub end of a cigar tucked in the crook of his index finger. "You're not going to get this figured out by wearing a hole in the floor."

The older man could use his calming techniques all he wanted. Kelly John wasn't in any mood to be calmed or gentled or put out to pasture.

Not when it looked like what he was about to be was put down.

He paced the SG-5 ops center's huge horseshoe workstation from his own desk to Tripp Shaughnessey's and back. Again and again and again.

"Easy for you to say." Kelly John stopped, sniffed. Christ, but he smelled like a freakin' sewer. "You aren't the one who screwed up."

It was more than screwing up the mission and giving the upper hand to Spectra IT—the only ones with any reason to have Marian Diamonds bugged. The ones receiving the feed at the far end of the camera.

After what Tripp had gone through with the duo recently, that much was a given as far as Kelly John was concerned.

No, it was endangering the Smithson Group, jeopardizing everything Tripp, Julian and Christian, Mick and Eli and Harry had been working for, failing himself.

Failing Hank.

Hank crossed his arms over his chest and rocked back on his boot heels. "Kelly, you did your best."

His best hadn't been good enough. Not this time. A hell of a hard pill to swallow considering the reason Hank had picked him to join the Smithson Group in the first place.

"Spectra had to know I was coming." And he'd shoot

himself for that if it would help. "That's the only way the timing of that camera install makes sense."

"They were protecting their assets," Hank reminded him.

A reminder that pissed off Kelly John even further when he thought of the source of the organization's millions. "Yeah, well, now they've got video proving how insecure they really are. And how stupid I really am."

Hank moved, blocking Kelly John's path, commanding his attention. "We'll figure it out, son. We'll figure it out."

"What's to figure?"

At Tripp Shaughnessey's offhanded question, both men turned, Kelly John glaring down at his partner where Tripp sat on the floor in front of his desk. "What the hell's that supposed to mean?"

Tightening the wheels on his upended chair, Tripp shrugged. "You're the techno whiz. Make your own video. Prove you were elsewhere at the time. Show them they only think they know what they're seeing."

"An alibi," Hank said.

Intrigued, Kelly John started pacing again. "That might work."

"And we all know who makes the best alibi for a man, right?" Tripp asked.

Kelly John knew he wasn't going to like the answer. "Who?"

"A woman."